Sea City, Here We Come!

Sea City, Here We Come!
Ann M. Martin

AN
APPLE
PAPERBACK

SCHOLASTIC INC.
New York Toronto London Auckland Sydney

Cover art by Hodges Soileau

Interior illustrations
by Angelo Tillery

ISBN 0-590-45674-1

12 11 10 9 8 7 6 5 4 3 2 1   3 4 5 6 7 8/9

Printed in the U.S.A.   40

First Scholastic printing, July 1993

*The author gratefully acknowledges
Peter Lerangis
for his help in
preparing this manuscript.*

Sea City, Here We Come!

Dear Keisha,

Guess what? I'm going to the Jersey shore for the first two weeks in August! I got a job taking care of the Pike kids with Mallory. They have this vacation house in Sea City, and it's right on the beach. Like, step out the front door and into the sand!

They were thinking of taking one of the older babysitters, but Mal convinced them to let me go. I am going to be the best sitter they ever dreamed of!

Love
Your best cousin,
Jessi

Mary Anne,
    Hi! Sorry I haven't written lately. Baseball season was a killer. I hurt my finger throwing a curve ball, so I spent the first week of summer vacation soaking it in pickle brine. (My finger, not the ball.) Anyway, enough said about your favorite sport. (Ha.ha.)
    What's up? Are you going to Sea City this summer? I am! I'm going to be a mother's helper. Toby's going to be there, too.
    Write back, okay? Hope I see you at the beach!
                        Your friend,
                            Alex
P.S. Is Stacey going to Sea City? Toby wants to know!

Deer Kristy
Were on vacation alredy. So Linnie and I cant come to Crushers practis this summer. Because dad had to take off earlier. I yeled and cried but it didnt matter. Linny's pretty angry.

                        From,
                        Hannie

2

Dear Dad,

How's July in the Big Apple? Catching any rays on the way to the E train? Just kidding! But next time I C U I'll be BRONZE! (I hope.) Mrs. Barrett's renting a house in Sea City near the Pikes, and she asked me if I could go along to help take care of her kids. I said, "Twist my arm!" No, really, I told her I'd ask permish. Mom says OK. Do you, too? (You do, right?)

Can't wait to hear.

LUV, Stacey

STONEYBROOK PUBLIC SCHOOLS
STONEYBROOK MIDDLE SCHOOL
ELM STREET
STONEYBROOK, CT

Dear Ms. Kishi
We are looking forward to seeing you at summer school.

Please report to room Gym at the high school, at 9:00 a.m. on Monday, July 1.

Sincerely,
Benjamin Taylor
Principal

3

Hi, Dad! Hi, Jeff!

Can't wait to see you at the end of Aug. I will have SO much to tell you by then. Here's why. This month, Mary Anne and I are going to run a summer Mini-Camp for the neighborhood kids! Now for the great news. The Pikes have invited Kristy, Claudia, Mary Anne, and ME to their beach house for one whole week in August! Yea! And Jessi, Mal, and Stacey will already be there. SEA CITY, HERE WE COME!

Oh. Can you think of a better name for our Mini-Camp? Richard suggested "Club Mad" (for Mary Anne and Dawn), but we said NO WAY! Anyway, eight kids have signed up already.

Save some CA sun for me!

Kisses & hugs,
Dawn

Dearest Stacey,

Have a fabulous time at
the beach. Just make
sure to bring back some
saltwater taffy for your
old man.

Love,
Hot, sweltering Dad

CHAPTER 1

Kristy

Friday

Dear Aunt Colleen & Uncle Wallace,
    What a busy July! Krushers' summer
season is already almost over. (Whew!)
Also, the BSC had its last _full_
meeting today. Three members are
going on vacation tomorrow. The
rest of us are going in a week.
So the next postcard you get from
me will be from... Sea City! I
am totally psyched. Say hi to
Ashley, Berk, Grace, & Peter!
                    XXX OOO
                    Kristy

"Sweet," Claudia Kishi said. "With a mild crunch and kind of a nutty aftertaste."

Jessi Ramsey nodded. "It gets nice and crumbly in your mouth. But it doesn't have the same . . . *burst* of flavor."

"The ingredients are definitely inferior," Logan Bruno added.

We sat, chewing thoughtfully, saying nothing. We looked like nine cows in a pasture.

"Okay, let's vote," Claudia said. "All those in favor of Sample A, raise your hands. . . . Sample B?"

No, we were not having some gourmet food sampling. It was minutes before our Friday Baby-sitters Club meeting, and Claudia was conducting an End-of-the-Season Junk Food Blind Taste-Off. We were to decide which tasted better, Heath Bars or Skor Bars. She had bought several of each and removed the wrappers so we wouldn't know which we were eating.

Strange, huh? That's Claudia. She's the BSC's resident junk food addict. Her bedroom (our official headquarters) is crammed full of candy, chips, and pretzels. And it's all well hidden, because her parents are firm believers in Good Nutrition. (They're also believers in Fine Literature, which is why Claudia has

7

also tucked her Nancy Drew books in among her socks and underwear.)

Claud is a talented artist, sculptor, and jewelry-maker. Mr. and Mrs. Kishi approve of those things, so Claud keeps her supplies in full view. Which is how she prevents her parents from finding her hidden stuff. She tells them no one's allowed to touch her works in progress — which occupy every corner of the room.

You can probably picture the place. It's a pigsty. (Sorry, but it is.) Us BSCers put up with it, though. One, because we love Claud. And two, because she's the only one of us who has her own private phone with a private phone number. (The phone is crucial to the success of our business.)

Here's how our club works. We meet Monday, Wednesday, and Friday afternoons from 5:30 to 6:00. During those times, we take calls from neighborhood parents who need sitters. We have seven members (nine, if you count our associates). So our clients know they can book a reliable, expert sitter with just one call.

The BSC was an idea waiting to happen. (I read that expression somewhere, and it really fits.) Actually, it was *my* idea. I thought of it awhile ago when my mom was having trouble lining up a sitter. And it has really worked. Now we have tons of regular clients. We keep them, too, because we're a well-run organization (also because we happen to be nice and charming and responsible).

Like any company, we have officers and rules and record-keeping. I'm the president. I run the meetings and plan special events for our charges. I also try to think up new publicity ideas.

In case you can't tell, I'm kind of a loudmouth. (But lovable, too.) Here are some other things about me: I love sports and animals, and I *live* in casual clothes such as jeans and sweats. Some of the others (Stacey, for instance) tease me about my lack of "fashion." I guess I could have lots of chic outfits if I wanted them (my stepdad is pretty rich), but I can't be bothered. I'd probably just mess them up, anyway.

My stepdad, by the way, is named Watson Brewer. My mom married him a year or so ago. (My father walked out on our family when I was seven. It's something I don't like to talk about.) Watson must really love kids, because when he married her, he got me and my three brothers in the bargain. (Charlie's seventeen, Sam's fifteen, and David Michael's seven.) Plus he has two kids from a previous marriage, named Karen and Andrew, who live with him every other weekend. Then, to top it all off, Mom and Watson adopted a little

Vietnamese girl named Emily Michelle (who just happens to be the cutest child in the universe). Then my grandmother moved in to help out. Now *that's* a big family. Not that space is a problem. Our house is this huge old mansion way on the other side of town. It's so far from Claud's, Charlie has to drive me to and from BSC meetings.

I *used* to live across the street from the Kishis, before Mom remarried. I've known Claudia since we were both in diapers. Even then she liked sweets. I *still* can't figure out how she stays so thin. Yes, Claudia the junk food fanatic has a figure like a model. She also has perfect skin. She's Japanese-American, with gorgeous black hair and almond-shaped eyes. And she can throw together the funkiest clothes and make them look good. That Friday, for instance, she was wearing ripped cut-off jeans held up by a frayed rope belt, a T-shirt with the collar torn off, huge white socks all bunched around the ankle, and old-fashioned black lace-up shoes. She looked totally cool.

Claud is our vice-president (mainly because we hold our meetings in her room). Her duties are answering the phone during non-meeting times and destroying our diets.

Although Claudia is one of my oldest friends, my *best* friend is Mary Anne Spier.

People say we look a little alike (we're both short and we both have shoulder-length brown hair), but we're opposites in many ways. Mary Anne hates anything athletic. Also she's the shyest, most sensitive person I ever met. She cries all the time. At movies, *some* people cry at the sad parts. Mary Anne can tell when the sad parts are coming, and starts crying *in advance*.

To tell you the truth, I'd probably be sensitive, too, if my mom had died when I was a baby. Mary Anne was sent away to live with her grandparents until her dad recovered from the loss. Eventually Mr. Spier took her back and raised her by himself. He was extremely strict. Mary Anne had to dress in little-girl clothes and wear her hair in pigtails until seventh grade. But that's all in the past now. Mr. Spier has loosened up a lot (I'll tell you why later). Now Mary Anne definitely looks her age. *And* she happens to be the only member of the BSC who has a steady boyfriend! He's Logan Bruno, an associate of the club, and he's cute and athletic and funny and all those good things. He also has this cool Southern accent.

Mary Anne is the BSC secretary. She handles our official record book — which includes our schedule of sitting jobs, an up-to-date client list, notes about our charges' special

11

needs, and a record of fees that each client pays. Mary Anne also keeps track of our own personal schedules (Jessi has regular ballet classes, Claudia takes art lessons, Mal goes to the orthodontist — stuff like that). She writes in this extra neat handwriting, and she's never made a mistake. Talk about organized.

"Okay, it's official," Claudia announced. "Sample A wins four to three, with two undecideds!" She turned over an index card that said SAMPLE A. The other side said SKOR.

Oh, by the way, all nine members were there, including our associates. That's unusual for us, but Claud's room is big enough — just barely.

"Hey, Skor scores!" Logan said.

"Congratulations," Stacey mumbled, chomping on some corn chips.

You may have noticed that two people didn't vote in the taste test. The "two abstentions" were for our health-food freaks, Stacey McGill and Dawn Schafer. Personally, I think health foods are for the birds (I mean that literally). Poor Stacey is *required* to stay away from sweets. She has diabetes, which means her body can't handle sugar. Because of that, she has to give herself (are you sitting down?) *injections* of something called insulin, every day.

Stacey is our treasurer. She collects weekly dues, which we use to help pay Claudia's phone bill, buy supplies, and contribute to my brother Charlie's gas expenses. Stace is also our resident New Yawka (she doesn't talk like one, though). She moved here last year when her dad's company transferred him. Then she moved back to NYC when her dad's company transferred him back. Then she moved here *again*, but without her father. Yes, unfortunately, it was the big D. Divorce. Now she and her mom live in Stoneybrook in a small house (Stacey's an only child).

Stacey's really beautiful. And sophisticated (but *not* snobby). And smart (especially in math). Plus she is the BSC's other fashion expert. She doesn't look a thing like Claud, though. Stacey has long blonde hair and blue eyes. She also has a sleeker, fancier style of dressing. Store-bought sensational, not thrown-together sensational like Claud. At our Friday meeting she was wearing this white T-shirt that hung practically to her knees (Stacey calls it a "jersey tunic" or something), white stretch pants ("ribbed leggings") to midcalf, a tan leather belt over the T-shirt, and leather-strap sandals. Sometimes Stacey likes to wear all black, which seems kind of weird in the summer.

While we're on the subject of "weird," let me tell you about our other health-food person, Dawn Schafer. (*She's* not weird, just her

13

taste in food.) Now, she doesn't have diabetes, so she *can* eat candy. But she just *doesn't*. She actually prefers health food. Stick a lump of tofu in front of her and she's happy. I have actually seen her turn down a steaming hot slice of pepperoni pizza for an avocado-and-greens sandwich on pita bread. Honest.

Needless to say, Dawn is a real individualist. She stands up for what she calls her "alternate life-style." Maybe that's why she's our alternate officer. (Her job is to fill in whenever one of us is absent.)

Dawn has amazing hair. It's super long, and so blonde it's almost white. She moved to Stoneybrook last year from Southern California. She also comes from a divorced family. Her dad and her younger brother still live near Los Angeles. Her mom is this beautiful, absent-minded woman who does things like leaving car keys in the linen closet.

Now get this. Both Dawn's mom and Mary Anne's dad have remarried — to each other! That's right. It turned out that they were sweethearts ages ago in Stoneybrook High School. They started dating again when Dawn and her mom moved here. So now free-spirited Sharon Schafer and stodgy Richard Spier live under the same roof — and so do Mary Anne and Dawn, as stepsisters.

And *that's* one reason Mr. Spier has loosened up. At least that's my theory.

Our junior officers, Jessica Ramsey and Mallory Pike, come from more typical families. (If there is such a thing as a typical family. Well, I take that back. The Pikes have eight kids, including triplets. *Jessi* comes from a more typical family, with one younger brother and one younger sister.

Jessi and Mal are both eleven years old and in sixth grade (the rest of us are thirteen-year-old eighth-graders). Their parents don't let them stay out late during the week, so they mostly take afternoon jobs. That works out well, because it frees up the rest of us for later jobs. Jessi and Mal are great sitters — and best friends. Both of them are into books, and they both complain that their parents treat them like babies. And they're both creative. Mal writes stories and illustrates them, and Jessi's an excellent ballerina (she takes lessons in Stamford, the nearest big city to Stoneybrook).

Physically they're nothing like each other. Jessi's black, and she has the long, long legs of a dancer. Mal is white, with red hair and normal legs. Mal also wears glasses and braces (the clear kind).

That leaves our associate officers. I already mentioned Logan, so I'll tell you a little about Shannon Kilbourne. She lives in my neighborhood and goes to Stoneybrook Day School, a private school. She has lots of interests, so she belongs to a million after-school clubs. Late this school year, her music teacher convinced Shannon that she could sing.

Which she had started doing in Claud's room, along with some hand gestures that I supposed were dance movements.

"Yoo-ee-yoo-ee-yoo-ee-yoo-ee," sang Shannon in a very soft voice.

At this point, my eyes were on Claud's digital clock. It read 5:29.

"Uh, Shannon," Claudia finally said. "Are you all right?"

Click. 5:30. "This meeting will come to order!" I announced.

Shannon stopped yoo-eeing.

"Any new business?" I asked.

No one answered for a moment. Then Claudia said, "I am dying to know what Shannon was doing."

Shannon smiled. "Just some vocal warm-ups. You know, for drama camp. Musical rehearsals start this week."

"Did they give you a part yet?" Jessi asked.

"Ado Annie in *Oklahoma*," Shannon replied.

"You are so lucky," Claudia said. "I mean, to be doing something *fun* this summer."

"You're all going to Sea City, right?" Shannon asked. "That's fun."

"Only Mal and Jessi and Stacey are going tomorrow," Claudia said. "The rest of us are going next week with Mrs. Barrett's fiancé, Franklin. And *I* have to suffer through five more days of summer school."

"Yuck," Shannon said.

"I still can't believe I'm so stupid in math that I had to go. I mean, if you do terrible in art class, or music, they don't make you go to summer school." Claudia sighed. "I'm depressed. Time for some Twinkies."

She jumped off her bed and plunged into the closet. When she came out, she was holding a shoebox full of Twinkies.

As we grabbed and ripped wrappers and munched, the phone rang.

Claudia swallowed quickly and picked up the receiver. "Hello, Baby-sitters Club. . . . Oh, hi, Myriah! You want to talk to her? Okay." She held the phone to Mary Anne.

"Hi, Myriah," said Mary Anne. "The last day is Friday. . . . No, it'll be over in time. Don't worry, I worked it out with Kristy. You can play. Okay, 'bye."

When she hung up, she turned to me and said, "Myriah was worried that Mini-Camp would conflict with the Krushers game."

"She's always worried about that," I replied. "It shows she's interested."

"You should have seen her yesterday at

17

Mini-Camp," Mary Anne said. "She drew this box on the side of the barn and spent half the day trying to throw a ball inside the lines."

"The strike zone," I informed her. (See what I mean about Mary Anne and sports?)

"Uh-huh," Mary Anne replied. "Only she brought Chewy that day and he kept chasing after the ball." (Chewy is short for Chewbacca, the Perkinses' Labrador retriever.)

Dawn laughed. "Then we had 'art corner,' and Chewy decided to whack his tail into the paint bottles."

"We got the paint off the patio," Mary Anne added. "But the grass looks sort of tie-dyed."

"It's been fun, though," Dawn said. "I'll be so sad to see Mini-Camp end."

Mary Anne sighed. "Yeah . . ."

I knew the waterworks were about to start. So I piped up, "Well, the Krushers are looking good. Only a week till our big showdown."

Our final opponents were going to be Bart's Bashers. As usual. (They're practically the only team we play.)

The Krushers and the Bashers are sort-of homemade teams. I organized the Krushers with kids who were too young or too afraid to play Little League or T-Ball. I'm not sure why Bart Taylor organized his team. (Bart is a very important topic. Much more on him later.)

"Too bad we have to miss it," Mal said.

"Yeah, it'll be really tough to be at the beach," I replied.

"Soaking up rays," Dawn said.

"Swimming," Claudia chimed in.

"Meeting cute lifeguards," Shannon added.

Mallory giggled. "Oooh, I can't *wait!*"

"Me neither!" Jessi squealed. "I am soooo excited. Your parents were so nice to let me come. I'm going to be the best mother's helper ever."

Stacey sighed. "You know, I kind of wish I were going to the Pikes' instead of the Barretts'. I'll feel so strange being down there in a different house."

"Don't worry, Stace," Mary Anne said. "You'll do great. Besides, you'll be next door to us. All the kids'll be playing together."

"I wonder if I'll run into you-know-who," Stacey said.

Mary Anne looked down and cleared her throat. "You will."

"That guy's going to be down there? The one who dumped Stacey?" I blurted out. (Tactful as usual.)

"Yeah," Mary Anne said. "I got this letter from Alex. He said Toby has a job as a mother's helper."

Stacey rolled her eyes. "Oh, groan. The last person I want to see."

I glanced at Logan. He did *not* look happy

when Mary Anne mentioned Alex. See, the last time Mary Anne was in Sea City, she and Alex became pretty friendly. It didn't turn into anything serious, though, just a couple of casual dates. Mary Anne is the loyal type — and Logan is *not* the jealous type. Still, I could tell Alex wasn't Logan's favorite topic.

The room had fallen silent. I thought fast. I knew Logan was working part-time at the Rosebud Cafe this summer. I also knew the Pikes had invited him to Sea City the next weekend. So I said, "I bet you'll be happy to get away from your job for a couple of days."

Logan's tense expression melted away. "Yeah," he said, smiling at Mary Anne. "I can't wait."

Mary Anne smiled back. "Me neither."

I, Kristy Thomas, had done my good deed for the day.

Too bad I couldn't make Stacey feel better.

CHAPTER 2

Claudia

Friday

Dear Stacey,
    By the time this card arrives, you will be at Sea City! Yea! I am soooooo jellous! But I miss you! Except Im going to see you in about an hour at the meting.... ?????? But when you read this, I will be missing you.
    Are you having a good time? I hop so. Me, I am counting the days til sumer school is over! I can do that now — count. See what a enducational experiense its been?
    Mabe when I com down we can have a bon fire. Then I will finly have a perfict use for my math notebook!
                                   Love, Claudia

Claudia

It was brutal.

Going to summer school, I mean. Let's face it, it's bad enough just to *have* to go. For me it was especially embarrassing, because of my sister. Her name is Janine. I call her Janine the Genius. And she is one. Her I.Q. is high enough for two people. She can do math problems in her sleep. Janine was going to summer classes, too — but they were at Stoneybrook University, and she was taking them because she *wanted* to. (My parents, of course, think Janine can do no wrong.)

Then there's summer school itself. They bunch all the grades into one place, the high school. Half the kids are these huge sixteen- and seventeen-year-olds who don't want to be there — and look much bigger and angrier than you. And the other half are little kids who don't want to be there — and walk around with these pathetic, scared faces.

I thought a long time about it. Now I have this theory. The Claudia Kishi Theory of Summer School Torture. See, the teachers like to take summers off, too. So the worst thing in the world is to have stupid kids in school. The kids have to make up classes, which means some teachers have to *teach* the classes.

If *you* were a teacher who had to give up a

vacation for summer school, how would you feel? I know I'd be furious.

So that's why they make summer school the most miserable place in the world: REVENGE!

I guess they figure they'll scare you into getting good grades the next year. They make it so horrible you'll never want to come back. Like prison.

Who knows, next summer they may have a rock pile.

I did end up working *hard*. I even understood the stuff.

Anyway, my class lasted for a month. The first week I felt as if I were in another town. I knew *nobody*. Everyone looked so glum and unfriendly.

The second week I got to know some of the kids. And you know what? Most of them were pretty cool.

Monday of that week, a bunch of us stopped at the ice cream truck on the way home. "Now let's see," said this girl named Theresa, as we walked with our pops. "If the guy has twenty-two ice cream bars that cost him fifty cents each, sells one to each of us for a dollar fifty, then . . . how much did his toupee cost?"

I nearly spit out my ice cream. "Stop!"

"Can we use a calculator?" asked another classmate, named Carly.

We laughed all the way home. The more we joked about how stupid we were, the closer we felt.

It turned out Carly lives near me. Over the week we became pretty good friends. She's a fantastic watercolorist and potter. She even has a pottery wheel in her basement.

You know what the best thing was? Eventually the kids in my class started calling me "the smart one." *Me.* Claudia, the Blot on the Kishi Family Tree.

So the good news was that despite the Torture Theory, and despite the fact that I *hated* the work, summer school actually wasn't so bad.

By the Friday of the BSC meeting, I was having mixed feelings. I was glad school was almost over, but I wondered what would happen to my new friendships. What if Carly and Theresa and I weren't in the same classes in the fall? Most of us were starting to feel pretty sad — especially Carly. I could sense she knew how strong my BSC friendships were.

I tried not to think of the future. And I vowed I'd write to Carly when I was on my *real* vacation.

It was hard to stay in a good mood at the BSC meeting. There was Shannon, on the way to stardom at summer camp. Jessi, Mal, and Stacey were a day away from fun and sun. Mary Anne and Dawn were all starry-eyed about Mini-Camp. And Kristy was her usual gung-ho self about the Krushers.

Thank goodness I was going to Sea City. I kept thinking about that. Every time I'd picture Jessi or Stacey or Mal on the beach, I'd just put myself in the picture.

Only eight days and counting! I could practically feel the ocean breezes.

But first I'd have to say good-bye to the others. When Saturday came, Kristy, Mary Anne, Dawn, and I met at the Pikes' house.

Do you know what it's like when a family of ten is leaving for vacation? It gives *chaos* new meaning. It's like cattle-rustling in an old Western.

Except cattle are much quieter than the Pike kids.

Jessi had slept over the night before. As I walked up the Pikes' lawn, she struggled out of the house with two suitcases.

She smiled and said, "Hi, Clau — "

Claire barreled out of the house. "Where's Thomas?"

"Who's Thomas?" Jessi asked.

"My new stuffed bear," Claire whined. "I can't find him!"

25

"Did you pack him?"

"I don't know."

"Let's check." Jessi put the suitcases down on the front stoop and opened one.

At that moment Margo's voice screamed from inside, "*Stop*, Nicky!"

I could hear her footsteps go *tap-tap-tap-tap-tap-tap* —

"Watch it!" Jessi cried.

Margo had run out the front door. The *tap*s stopped when her foot landed inside Claire's open suitcase.

"No!" shouted Claire.

"Whoa!" shouted Margo.

Margo went flying onto the lawn. Claire's suitcase followed her, spilling clothes and toys and books. Jessi ran to Margo. I rushed over to help. Nicky appeared in the door, his mouth hanging open.

"Are you okay?" Jessi and I asked Margo at the same time.

"Did Nicky touch me?" was her reply.

"I *didn't*," Nicky said.

Margo burst into tears. "He was trying to lick me and give me his cootie germs!"

Jessi and I looked at each other, then at Nicky. By now, most of the other Pike kids — and Mr. Pike — had come to the door.

"Nicholas," Mr. Pike said very seriously.

"Please come into the living room. We need to have a talk."

"Oooh, Nicky," teased Adam. Or Byron. Or Jordan. (I wasn't really looking at them, so it was hard to tell. They're identical triplets.)

As Nicky slunk inside, Claire cried, "Here he is!" She held up a gray stuffed bear with a scarf around its neck.

"Thomas?" Jessi asked.

With a huge smile, Claire hugged the bear. "Thomas-silly-billy-goo-goo!"

She turned and began to skip into the house.

"Uh, Claire," Jessi said. "Would you help me pick up all this stuff?"

"*Margo* knocked it over," Claire replied.

"*Jessi* was the one who opened it on the stoop," Margo shot back.

For a moment — just a teeny moment — I was glad I was going to summer school instead of to Sea City.

Mal bustled out the front door with a couple more suitcases. "Uh-oh," she said. "Let's see if we can pack Claire's suitcase in world record time!"

Well, that seemed to do the trick. Everyone pitched in and stuffed the suitcase again.

Then the kids ran back into the house, screaming with excitement. Mal and Jessi and

I carried the suitcases to the cars.

"Hi!" Dawn called from down the street. She and Mary Anne were walking toward the house.

"Hi!" Jessi, Mal, and I called back.

Mary Anne pointed to a minivan in the Pikes' driveway. "Whose is that?"

"My mom and dad rented it," Mal replied.

Dawn looked puzzled. "But you have two station wagons."

"Well, we're bringing twelve people to Sea City," Mal said, pulling open the rear of the van. "And since you guys and Logan are all arriving next week with Franklin and his kids, and *they're* leaving with only Logan on Monday, that means we'll be coming home with . . . um . . ."

We counted in our heads. "Sixteen!" I announced. (See, summer school had done me some good.)

"Right," Mal said. "So Dad figured we would be more comfortable with a van and a station wagon."

Honk! Honk!

The Junk Bucket was turning into the driveway. That's the name of Charlie Thomas's car. Kristy was practically hanging out the window, waving.

Honestly, that car is so old and rusty and clankety, I don't know why it doesn't fall apart. (Kristy's rich neighbors must *love* it.)

" 'Bye!" Kristy yelled.

"We're not going yet!" Jessi reassured her.

When Kristy got out, Charlie tooted the horn a couple of times and headed back home.

The Pikes' door opened again, and the rest of the family came tromping out. They were carrying suitcases, backpacks, fishing gear, flippers, water wings, life vests, you name it.

"I call the van!" Adam yelled.

"Me too!" cried Nicky.

"Me too!" the rest of the kids screamed.

"I called first!"

"*I* did!"

Mr. Pike let out a whistle. In a loud voice, he announced who was going in which vehicle. Of course, this was followed by a chorus of "No fair!" and "Can we switch on the way back?" and "I'm hungry!"

Soon everyone was handing us stuff to pack into the car and van. Mr. and Mrs. Pike knew exactly how to stack everything to make it all fit.

Vanessa Pike stood next to us with an excited smile. That usually means she is about to recite a poem (Vanessa loves to speak in rhymes). "As we pack up for New Jersey," she said, "everything is topsy-turvy."

In the backseat of the station wagon, Nicky

groaned loudly. "That doesn't rhyme, mush-brain!" he cried.

Vanessa put her hands on her hips. "Sticks and stones may break my bones — "

"And we all hate your stupid poems!" Adam bellowed from the van.

"*That* doesn't rhyme, either!" Vanessa retorted.

"If there is any more fighting, we are *not* stopping for ice cream," Mrs. Pike said. "Now come on!"

Before long, we were finished packing and the kids were in the car. Then Stacey came jogging over from the Pikes' backyard. (She and her mom live in the house behind the Pikes'.) "Hi, guys," she said. "I came to say good-bye. The Barretts are going to pick me up in a few minutes."

On her face was this half-happy, half-sad expression. I could see Mary Anne's lips start to quiver. "Oh . . ." she said. "I'll miss you!"

"Me too!" Stacey replied. She and Mary Anne hugged and rocked back and forth.

Then Mal and Jessi and I said, "Ohhhhh," and went into a three-way hug.

"Hey, we're only going to be separated for a week," said Kristy, the Voice of Sanity.

We agreed that Kristy was right. Eventually

Jessi hopped into the station wagon and Mal climbed into the van.

" 'Bye!" the rest of us called out as the caravan began moving. "See you soon!"

" 'Bye!" answered Jessi and a couple of the other kids (the rest were gabbing and fidgeting and getting tangled in seat belts).

"Tell Mrs. Barrett we'll meet her at the gas station!" Mrs. Pike called out.

"Okay!" I replied. We waved until they disappeared. Then we ran through the Pikes' yard to Stacey's house. Mrs. McGill was smiling, but looked a little worried. "Now, you packed your injection kit?" she asked.

"Yes, Mom," Stacey said patiently.

"And you have the number for the doctor down there, just in case?"

"Yes, Mom."

"We're hee-ere!" Buddy Barrett's voice shouted from the driveway.

Stacey looked at Mary Anne, Kristy, Dawn, and me. "Ohhh . . ."

We all hugged *again*. Mary Anne started bawling. To tell you the truth, I was a little misty-eyed myself (but maybe it was because I was thinking of summer school).

We followed Stacey to the front yard. She grabbed her suitcase, which was on the porch, and ran to the car. Mrs. Barrett helped her jam it into the trunk. We mentioned the gas station to Mrs. Barrett. She thanked us, climbed into the driver's seat, and pulled away.

The car jumped the curb, then drove onto the road.

" 'Byyyyeeee!" the cry rang out along Elm Street.

Sigh.

Some of us were on our way.

I felt pretty good, though. Because it meant *my* trip was that much closer!

CHAPTER 3

Mallory

Saturday

Hi, Dawn!

Well, we're here! What a trip. Everybody was so noisy. When we stopped for lunch, Nicky insisted on getting a large chocolate milkshake with extra ice cream. But only because the triplets each got one. Well, guess who barfed all over the rented van later on? It was gross. Dad had to drive to a car wash where they had a water hose and a wet vacuum. So the rest of the way the carpet was squishy and the van smelled. Everybody wanted to ride in the station wagon after that. Poor Nicky. (Poor us, too.)

Jessi says hi! More on the Pike saga tomorrow.

Miss ya,
Love, Mal

"One!" Vanessa squealed.

We were about an hour away from Stoney-brook. Vanessa, Nicky, and Claire had decided to play some sort of secret game. For a long time they'd been staring out the window. Now they were collapsing into giggles in their seats.

I hadn't been paying much attention to them. I was too busy reading my book, *The Golden Key* by George MacDonald, which was taking a lot of concentration.

"One what?" I said, looking up.

They all giggled again. I went back to my book.

About ten minutes later, Nicky blurted out, "Two!"

More hysterical giggles.

I happened to be looking out the window when they got to "Four." That was when I figured out what they were doing — counting people in other cars who were picking their noses.

So mature.

"Come on, let's play a new game," I suggested. "I'll start a story and everybody will add to it."

"Nooo," Nicky complained.

"Okay, you don't have to play, Nicky," I said. "Vanessa: Once upon a time there was

34

a big fat toad who ate something very strange. Your turn."

"Um . . . It was a goober from an old man with a bushy mustache!" she said, convulsing with laughter again.

"Then he turned green and sprouted hair from his ears!" Nicky added, suddenly interested.

"And went to the barber to have his ears cut off," Claire said.

We continued this until everyone was laughing too hard to go on.

Before long Vanessa asked, "When are we going to stop?"

"When we get past New York City," Dad said. "I agreed with Mom and Mrs. Barrett to stop at the Howard Johnson's, like we always do."

"If you had a car phone you could call them and tell them to stop now!" Nicky said, pouting.

"Which is why I don't have a car phone," Dad mumbled.

"What?" Nicky said.

"Oh, nothing," Dad replied. I smiled at him.

Well, getting past New York ended up taking a lifetime. We got stuck in traffic between two enormous trucks for about a half hour.

By the time we reached the Howard Johnson's, we were *starving*.

I guess that's why Nicky thought he could drink that humongous milkshake. I don't need to go into the gory details — except to say that the Pike Family Barf Bucket was in the *wrong* car for this trip.

I sat by the window after that. It seemed like the place to be after Nicky's little accident. But I'd forgotten about New Jersey's fragrant industrial area. It's miles and miles of huge metal tanks surrounded by spiral stairs and blinking lights. It looks like a convention of spaceships. And it smells like a sewer.

It was hard to say which was better, inside or out.

Vanessa made the most of the situation. She had new material for her poetry. "Mister Smee and Captain Hook, ran away from Nicky's puke!"

"Vanessa!" Dad said warningly from the front seat.

I gave her a Look. Nicky was curled up in his seat, trying to sleep it off. I went back to my book.

"Hurry up and get a scarf! Please wipe up this pile of — "

"*Vanessa!*" This time Dad and I yelled at the same time.

"Sto-o-o-p," Nicky moaned.

I thought the trip would never end. My eyes were just closing when Dad said, "Uh-oh, do you see what I see?"

I sat up. We were zooming past a familiar sign. " 'Sea City, Exit Ten Miles,' " I read aloud.

Claire started squealing. Vanessa screamed out, "Sea City, here we come!" Even Nicky came to life.

As we approached the Jersey shore, the scenery changed drastically. All these memories from past trips came back. The air became at least ten degrees cooler. I could smell the ocean. The dirt along the road was sandy and the trees were scrubby. Seagulls screeched overhead.

The kids were jumping with excitement when Dad drove off the exit ramp. We traveled a few minutes more and came to a huge, reedy marsh. Across the marsh was a loooong, narrow road, built up on a jetty of rocks all cemented together.

We knew that road well. It is the only way to get to Sea City.

"The bridge! The bridge!" Claire piped up.

"It's not a bridge," Vanessa corrected her. "It's a causeway. Here we go driving to the beach — "

"Hey, Vanessa," Nicky interrupted. "What rhymes with causeway?"

The van was silent for the next few minutes. I closed my eyes and breathed in the salty air.

Just over the causeway, a three-dimensional

purple cow loomed over the road on a billboard. That's our first important landmark
on the way to Sea City. "The cow!" Claire
shouted.

I pointed to our second landmark, a road-
side restaurant. "Crabs for Grabs!"

But the third landmark had changed. It used
to be a billboard for suntan lotion, which
showed a dog pulling down a little girl's
bathing suit. Now it was an ad for a new local
hot dog place.

"Loooook," Nicky said sadly, as if he'd just
been told Sea City had washed away forever.
"The tushy picture's gone."

"What does the sign say?" Claire asked.

" 'Weiner's Wieners,' " I read.

Well, that was good enough. The little girl's
bare bottom was instantly forgotten in a fit of
giggling.

Sea City is on a curved piece of land (a "spit"
of land, Dad calls it) that juts into the ocean
like a long tail. It seems like an island, but
technically it's not. There are patches of marsh
connecting it to the "mainland."

One time it *turned* into an island, though.
According to the Sea City guidebook, a huge
storm washed out the marsh and the causeway. But that was ages ago.

We zoomed onto Sea City's main road. Suddenly we were surrounded. Hot dog stands,

souvenir shops, umbrella rentals, seafood restaurants, fish markets. The crackling sound of frying food everywhere. "There's Trampoline Land!" Nicky shouted.

"And miniature golf!" Vanessa said.

In the distance I could see the huge Ferris wheel arcing over the boardwalk. And I could hear crashing sounds that could only be one thing — the ocean.

We had arrived. I couldn't wait to see our house.

A stiff breeze was blowing as we pulled into our driveway. I could tell because the wind chimes on the front porch were tinkling, and the white wicker swing was rocking back and forth.

I love our Sea City house. We rent the same one every year. It's Victorian-style, a big gingerbread cottage with yellow and white trim. There are gables and eaves and posts everywhere. And three whole floors.

You know what the best part is? It *faces* the ocean.

"Oooooh, honeysuckle, honeysuckle!" Vanessa cried, running to the blossoming bush.

"Makes me want to laugh and chuckle!" Nicky said. "Hey, Vanessa, did you hear that?"

Nicky was very proud of himself, but Vanessa was too busy sniffing away to pay attention.

The station wagon pulled up just moments later. "Let's go to the beach!" Adam and Margo were screaming.

"Let's unpack!" Mom answered.

I have to admit, it was hard to unload the car when the beach was staring us in the face. But this year I was not only the oldest Pike kid, I was a mother's helper (*parents'* helper would be more accurate).

Somehow Dad, Mom, Jessi, and I managed to help everybody settle in. Jessi and I staked out the yellow-wallpapered bedroom on the second floor, where Mary Anne and Stacey stayed when they had been parents' helpers last time.

"I *love* this view!" Jessi said, gazing out the window. Her grin was so big, I thought her face would crack. "I can't believe how beautiful Sea City is!"

"Hi, up there!"

We looked down to see Stacey with Buddy and Suzi Barrett (Buddy's seven and Suzi's five). "Hi!" we both called.

"We're going to claim the beach!" Buddy said.

"Us too!" cried some voices from below and above us. Instantly the Pike herd began stampeding. Their footsteps rattled the stairways.

"We better go," I said to Jessi.

In a few moments we found ourselves running through the sand toward the ocean.

I have never seen Jessi so happy. She was like a little kid, jumping and screaming.

Stacey had run ahead of us. She was already talking to two guys, near a couple of blankets close to the beach. A group of kids was busy digging sand castles nearby. Our charges quickly joined them.

Typical Stacey, I thought. She *would* find the guys right away. Once she had this huge crush on a lifeguard named Scott, who unfortunately had no interest in her. Then she met a boy named Toby. He was the cousin of a parents' helper named Alex. Alex and Mary Anne became good friends, and Stacey and Toby actually dated. But poor Stacey had bad luck again. He broke up with her at the end of the vacation.

I stopped in my tracks when I saw the guy's face. He *was* Toby. I remembered him. The same wavy brown hair, freckles, deep brown eyes . . .

Deep, *luscious* brown eyes. Wow, he was cute. I didn't remember *that* about him.

"So, you're going to be here awhile?" I heard him say to Stacey.

"Mm-hm," Stacey replied.

"Perfect tanning day," Toby said. "Huh?"

Stacey shrugged. "I guess." Then she looked away and shouted, "Suzi, stay back from the water!"

"Who's bringing Mary Anne down?" asked the other guy.

I tore my eyes away from Toby for a moment. The other guy was fairer-skinned and had lighter brown hair. It took me a minute to realize he was Alex.

"The boyfriend of the woman I'm working for," Stacey said. "Uh, excuse me." She went running off toward Suzi, who really wasn't doing anything unsafe, as far as *I* could see.

"Oh, hi," Toby said, looking at me. "I'm Toby and this is my cousin Alex. I don't think we've met."

"Mal," I said. "I mean, I'm Mallory Pike." My voice sounded as if I'd swallowed a fur ball.

Toby's eyes widened. "*Pike?* Are you one of the ones Stacey and Mary Anne used to sit for?"

I felt deflated. "Yeah. But now I'm sitting, too."

Toby seemed to find that funny. "I can believe that. You sure have changed."

"Well, it happens," I said, laughing.

"Yeah."

Soon we separated to watch our charges. But I could see Toby looking at me off and on during the afternoon. And smiling, too.

Could it be? It didn't seem possible. He was so much *older*. Fifteen, probably.

But I liked the way he was making me feel. I'd never felt that way before.

CHAPTER 4

Stacey

saturday

Dear Claud,

Sea City is beautiful. The weather is great. The kids are having a fantastic time.

Buddy wasn't too bad on the trip down. Did you know Mrs. Barrett is a nervous driver? Well, she is. Being in heavy traffic with her was NOT fun. The trip seemed REALLY long.

I don't know why, but today was harder work than I expected. Maybe it's just me. I saw <u>Toby</u> today (gag me!) and I think that got things off to a weird start.

Oh, well. I'm happy to be here. Really. And I can't wait for you to come.

Love,
Stacey

Stacey

Let me say it right out. I *hated* my first day at Sea City.

I don't know why I was being so polite in my card to Claudia. Maybe I thought someone at the Sea City post office would read it and tell Mrs. Barrett.

What I really wanted to say was this: Mrs. Barrett was being a big pain in the neck.

Usually I like her. For one thing, she is, like, stunning. She seems younger than a lot of moms. She wears the coolest clothes, which look great on her incredible, Cosmo-model figure. Her hair is a gorgeous chestnut color, with natural curls that spill to her shoulders. I would *love* to look like her when I'm older.

Her personality? Well, nice but disorganized. She's famous for calling the BSC during non-meeting times. Which isn't totally her fault. She's divorced and has to take care of three kids on her own. Buddy's the oldest, and he's a handful. He's a skinny eight-year-old who can't seem to sit still. His sister Suzi, who's five, is a cute little pudge who loves to play pretend. And Marnie's an adorable two-year-old with curly blonde hair and blue eyes.

I was looking forward to being her helper — and going to Sea City. But I felt a little funny not working for the Pikes. Twice before I'd gone to the beach with them, and I loved it.

I understood, though, that Mal was old enough now to be responsible, and Jessi's her best friend. And the Barretts' house was next door to the Pikes', so it wasn't as if I wouldn't see them.

Anyway, by the time we left Stoneybrook, I was totally psyched. Mrs. Barrett was excited and friendly when she picked me up. She kept thanking me for coming.

I should have known I was in for trouble when she drove onto the curb, just outside her house.

"Oh!" she cried. "What did I do?"

"My dad does that all the time," I said as the car bumped back onto the street. "He grew up in New York City, so he didn't get his license till he was in his twenties."

That little story is usually interesting to grown-ups. But Mrs. Barrett simply said "Mm-hm," and clutched the steering wheel tighter.

Just outside Stoneybrook, Buddy began asking, "When are we going to stop?"

"Buddy, can't you see I'm driving?" Mrs. Barrett snapped. "I have to follow the Pikes or we'll get lost."

I was sitting in the front. I turned around to face the kids. Marnie was already drifting off to sleep in her car seat. "Come on, Buddy and Suzi," I said. "Let's see who can spot the most out-of-state license plates."

I explained the game to Suzi. They played a pretty long time, but Mrs. Barrett's mood didn't improve.

Honnnnnnk! "Stay in your lane, you creep!" she yelled to someone who pulled in between her and the Pikes.

Scrreeeeek! She stomped on the brakes when someone swerved toward her from an entrance ramp. The car skidded a little, and she screamed.

Suzi shrieked. Buddy looked pale with shock. Marnie woke up crying. Mrs. Barrett said — well, I won't say what she said.

Things just went from bad to worse. We got stuck in a traffic jam on the highway by New York City. *And* we lost track of both Pike cars.

I reminded Mrs. Barrett we'd agreed to meet the Pikes at a Howard Johnson's in New Jersey. That made her feel a *little* better.

We did all catch up at the Howard Johnson's. But Marnie decided she wanted to live there. She absolutely, positively did not want to ride another minute in the car.

The problem was, we had a good hour to go.

And she didn't stop crying for even a second.

Then the Pikes had to get off the highway when Nicky barfed. Well, Mrs. Barrett went ballistic trying to figure out what was wrong. She was convinced we were lost.

By the time we reached the Sea City cause-way, Mrs. Barrett's knuckles were white around the steering wheel.

"I have to go to the bathroom!" Buddy cried.

"I want apple juice!" Suzi whined.

"Waaaaaaaaah!" Marnie shrieked.

I was a wreck. Even the purple cow didn't make me smile.

Next to the Pikes' house, the Barretts' looked tiny. And not nearly as old. It was a plain, white-shingled bungalow with chrysanthe-mums and rhododendrons growing in front. It looked as though it had been built on what had been the side yard of the Pikes' house.

But when we stepped inside, Mrs. Barrett became human again.

"Stacey, thanks for being so patient with me," she said as we were unpacking the suit-cases (the kids were busy changing into their swimsuits). "This is just such a new experi-ence for me. It's my first vacation as a single parent. It's the longest I've ever driven. It's the first time I've hired a mother's helper." She let out a deep breath, then smiled warmly. "I — I just feel a little overwhelmed, you know?"

I smiled back. "That's okay. Why don't I take the kids to the beach and give you a chance to rest?"

Her face brightened. "Thanks. Just don't forget the sun lotion."

I felt much better. I gathered the kids and slathered them with lotion (the old gather and slather). Then we ran to the Pikes'.

In minutes we were storming the beach together. The wind and sun felt *wonderful*. The sand tickled my feet. A wave broke on the shore, and I could feel its cool mist. My last bit of tension just melted away.

And that was when I saw Toby.

He tried to be so friendly. How could he even *face* me after dumping me? What nerve!

I was determined not to let him ruin my trip. I hardly said a word to him. I pretended the kids needed me and I ran away.

Toby's and my charges played together at first, then drifted apart. That was fine with me. I didn't look at him, didn't even *think* of him again.

Until suppertime.

As the kids ran back into the houses, screaming and laughing, Mal pulled me aside. "Uh, Stacey . . . are you and Toby, like, you know, still . . . ?"

"Mal," I said, "if a great white shark were to hop up on the beach and take him away, I wouldn't mind a bit."

Mal's eyes opened wide. "Really?"

"Well, I might feel sorry for the shark," I said. "Why?"

Mal giggled. "Well, um, it's just that . . . I think he likes me."

"Whaaaat?" I didn't mean to sound so surprised. I didn't mean to imply that Mallory wasn't attractive to guys. But I hadn't expected to hear her say that.

"He was so sweet to me, Stacey," she said. "And the way he was looking at me . . . I could just *tell* — "

I exhaled. "Mal, don't get your hopes up."

"What do you mean?" She looked crushed.

"Look, it's not that he *wouldn't* be interested in you. It's just . . . it's just *him*, that's all. He talks a good game, Mallory. He seems so cool and friendly. But if you ever got involved with him, you'd just get hurt. He'd dump you like he dumped me."

Mal's brow was furrowed. "Well, how do you *know*? I mean, maybe he's changed — "

I was losing my patience. The idea that that *dweeb* would flirt with an eleven-year-old made me furious. "Take my advice, Mal. Forget Toby. That's all I want to say. I have to help Mrs. Barrett with dinner."

I began to walk toward the house. I heard Mal say, "I think you're . . . you're *jealous*, Stacey."

Stacey

That made me turn around. I couldn't believe those words came out of Mallory Pike's mouth.

"What?" I said.

"If you don't like him anymore, then you shouldn't mind if he likes *me*," Mal went on. "Besides, just because I'm younger than you doesn't mean I'm a *baby*. I can take care of myself with boys!"

With that, she marched into her house.

And I marched into mine.

Mallory and Toby? This was the last thing I needed.

Dawn

Monday

Dear Jessi,
I think "Club Mad" might have been a good name for Mini-Camp, after all.
Today was going to be a fun, simple day. Collages, snack, and a visit to the Stones' farm. We had planned it so carefully.
It was a disaster. Worse than that, a fiasco (I think that's worse.) Well, whatever. Now, when you walk in our yard, your footsteps crunch. And poor Mrs. Stone is going to have to send her animals to a psychiatrist. I'd go into the details, but it'll be more fun to tell you in person.

FIVE MORE DAYS!!!!!!!!!
Oh, some good news. I
called Franklin to ask about
our ride, and he wants me
to sit for his kids next weekend.
That's all for now. Mary Anne
says hi.
          ↓   LUV, Dawn

Hi!

"**W**hich ones are hard-boiled?" I shouted, gazing into our refrigerator. I saw three egg cartons, neatly stacked on the bottom shelf.

"The two cartons on the right," Mary Anne called from the yard. She was busily setting up for the noon arrival of our Mini-Campers.

"But all three cartons are in one pile!" I replied.

"Oh, Dad must have restacked them," Mary Anne said. "Just take an egg from each and spin it."

"Huh?"

"Bring them all outside. I'll figure it out."

I picked up the cartons and walked out the back door. Mary Anne had placed our picnic table and a card table next to each other, side by side. On them was a stack of colored oak-tag; three bottles of Elmer's glue; containers filled with small seashells, sand, and un-cooked elbow macaroni; and some smaller empty containers. (We had gotten permission to take the sand from a neighborhood play-ground, and Mary Anne had collected the shells in Sea City.)

Today's first project was my idea, "Summer Collages." I figured it would be a great way to start our last week of Mini-Camp — impres-sions of the summer gone by and adventures yet to come.

Mini-Camp had been hard work, but a lot of fun. We'd done face-painting and "sand sculpture" (layers of colored sand in a small bottle), and taken a trip to the Stoneybrook Fire Department. We'd even had a dramatic presentation of the Dr. Seuss book, *The Lorax*. (I think environmental issues are really im-portant. If you don't know what *The Lorax* has to do with that, you should read the book.)

"What's this about spinning the egg?" I asked Mary Anne as I put the cartons on the picnic table.

"Watch." She took one from the top carton and spun it on its side. "That's hard-boiled." Then she took an egg from the carton under-neath and spun *that* one. It turned only once or twice, *very* wobbly. "That's raw. It does that because of the liquid inside."

I smiled. "You're a genius."

Mary Anne actually blushed. I carefully replaced the raw egg. Before I could take the carton inside, I heard a voice scream out, "Hiiii!"

We turned to see Jenny "Our Angel" Prezzioso running toward us. She's a four-year-old who lives next door, and she's one of our campers. ("Our Angel" is what her parents call her, but she *isn't*. She's kind of spoiled.)

"Hi!" Mary Anne and I both called back.

"What are we doing today?" Jenny asked.

I put the carton down and began to explain the project. Soon the other kids started filtering in: first Myriah Perkins, who's five; Jamie Newton (four); Charlotte Johanssen (eight); and Mathew and Johnny Hobart (six and four).

"Okay," Mary Anne announced, "today we're making summer collages. We have things here you can use. But first you have to find your own materials. Take the empty containers and go collect some natural objects that you can glue to your papers."

"Things that remind you of summer and Mini-Camp," I added.

The kids grabbed the containers and took

off. Charlotte came back first, with grass clippings, leaves, a dandelion, and some twigs. She got to work with the Elmer's glue.

Before long all the kids were at their places, gluing away. Mary Anne sat beside them, breaking some hard-boiled eggs. She put the inside parts into one container (to be used for egg salad later) and the shells into another. "You can use the sand, elbow macaroni, and eggshells for different textures," she said.

Mathew Hobart was holding two small seashells over his eyes. Before I could figure out what he was doing, he'd managed to hold them in place by lowering his eyebrows over them. "Hi!" he said, turning blindly to his left and right.

Well, everyone hooted with laughter. The kids tried to copy him. "Come on, guys," Mary Anne said, "some of those edges are — "

"Owwwwww!" Jamie Newton cried. A tiny trail of blood began to sprout from a cut high on his right cheek.

"Ooh, let me clean that off," Mary Anne said.

As they walked inside, I heard a *splat* behind me.

I turned to see Myriah Perkins staring at her

collage. A broken raw egg was spreading across it. "Ooops," she said. "I thought they were hard-boiled."

Well, we all shrieked about *that*. Myriah had taken the liberty of reaching into the nearest egg carton (left there by yours truly).

The kids were giddy now. Johnny began pouring Elmer's glue on top of the egg.

"Eww!" Marilyn, Myriah, and Jenny yelled.

"Johnny, no!" I said.

Crunch. Jenny had sat on . . . something. She'd stopped laughing. Slowly she stood up and looked underneath her.

Another egg was there. This one was hard-boiled. And squashed into a white-and-yellow mishmash.

Mathew was laughing so hard he fell to the ground.

"Mathew Hobart," I scolded, "did you do that?"

"I'm going to tell!" Jenny said. "My bottom's going to be all *yucky*."

The kids were gone. On another planet. Even Charlotte was laughing, and she's the most mature, serious kid I know.

I could see it was time to move on. I helped wipe off the back of Jenny's shorts. As soon as Mary Anne returned, I said, "Uh, I think we should go to the Stones'."

Jamie seemed to be fine. He even looked

proud of the little Band-Aid on his cheek. Mary Anne said, "I'll call Mrs. Stone to make sure it's okay to come early."

Johnny was now pretending a clump of grass was a mustache. Myriah was trying to make elbow macaroni into fangs. Charlotte, of course, was making a beautiful collage.

"She says it's okay!" Mary Anne said, running out of the house. "Let's go see the animals!"

"Yeaaa!"

We left for our Mini-Camp Day at the Farm. (This was Mary Anne's idea, and a great one.) Down the road from us is an actual small farm, owned by this friendly couple, Mr. and Mrs. Stone. They have the cutest baby goat named Elvira, and guess what? Mary Anne and I actually goat-sat Elvira for a few days when the Stones were out of town.

It's a loooong walk, all the way past the cemetery on the outskirts of town. But the kids were so excited they didn't mind. They began running when they heard Mrs. Stone call, "Hello, kids!" from her driveway.

Of course, we all wanted to see Elvira first. "Ooooh, hi, cutie!" Mary Anne said, scooping her up.

The kids squealed about how cute Elvira is. And it's true. She's a scrawny little bundle of hair and knees and elbows, with this pointy chin and big, big eyes.

"Are you kids hungry?" Mrs. Stone asked.

"Yeah!" cried Myriah and Jamie.

"Is peanut butter and jelly all right?"

"Yeah!" (See what I mean about Mrs. Stone being nice?)

She returned a few minutes later with a platter stacked with all the ingredients for p.b. & j. sandwiches.

"Thank you," I said as she set it down on her picnic table. I found a plastic knife and went to work.

Behind me, three different-sized dogs wandered around the yard, along with a fat goose. "Who's that?" I asked.

"Glynis," Mrs. Stone said. "She thinks she's a dog."

"Oh," I said with a laugh. I could tell the kids were in heaven. Myriah was heading toward the Stones' small pasture, where they keep four cows. Jamie was peeking into the pig pen. Mathew and Johnny were —

"Oh! Oh! Oh! Oh!"

That was Jenny, by the barn. Elvira was trying to get behind her. She seemed determined to butt her in the behind.

"Help! Help!" Jenny cried.

Mary Anne and I both rushed to her, but Mrs. Stone got there first. "Bad girl!" she said, pulling Elvira away by the collar.

Jenny was bawling. "I want to go *home!*"

"Honey, do you have anything in your back pocket?" Mrs. Stone asked.

"Waaahh! No!" Jenny cried.

I suddenly realized what had happened. Elvira had smelled the smushed egg on Jenny's pants.

"Here, doggie! Here, doggie!" Johnny was chasing after Mrs. Stone's Labrador retriever with a stick.

"Johnny," I said, "put the stick d — "

ROWWWRF! The dog lunged at Johnny. Johnny screamed and jumped away, bumping into Mathew. Mathew stumbled on Glynis the goose. Glynis let out a honk, spread her wings, and ran toward Charlotte.

Charlotte turned chalk white. "Aaaaaah!"

I ran to Charlotte and gave her a hug (Glynis was walking around as if nothing had happened). Mary Anne was holding Jenny up off the ground, comforting her. Mrs. Stone was in the barn, putting Elvira into her pen. Mathew and Johnny were rubbing their sores. And Myriah and Jamie were holding their stomachs, laughing.

"It's not *funny*," Johnny said.

"Uh, why don't we have snack?" I suggested.

We sat on the picnic bench. Mrs. Stone returned and said, "Don't you worry. Elvira's in her pen. The other animals won't hurt you."

"Thank you, Mrs. Stone," I said.

We wandered around a little more after our snack. No major tragedy occurred, until Jamie offered the half-empty peanut butter jar to Elvira. She plunged her snout right in, and it got stuck.

With a sharp fling, she sent the jar across the barn.

CRASSSSSH! It smashed into pieces on the cement floor.

"Beeeeeaahh!" Elvira complained.

"It's okay, that's easily cleaned!" Mrs. Stone called out.

I couldn't believe how cheerful she was. But I knew the cheerfulness wasn't going to last forever.

Neither Mary Anne nor I wanted to wait around until it ran out. We politely thanked her and walked back home with our campers.

When the day finally ended, Mary Anne and I collapsed on the front lawn.

"What a day!" was my gross understatement.

"Only four more after this," Mary Anne said.

We both sighed and looked away.

Finally I spoke up. "You know, we really

should plan some special activity for our last day."

"Something clean and easy," Mary Anne suggested. "Like storytelling."

"Or a trip to the mall," I said.

"How about a movie?"

Then I thought of a sleepover I had organized once. It had been a fundraiser for some pen pals of the elementary school kids, and everyone had had a great time. "Why don't we have an overnight, under the stars?"

"Are you serious?" Mary Anne said. "After what happened today? It's hard enough to control the kids when it's light outside."

"We don't have to do anything fancy," I said. "Can you imagine how cute they'd be — climbing into their sleeping bags with their little pj's, watching for shooting stars, telling ghost stories . . ."

"Yeah, but I don't know. It would be a lot of work."

I could tell she was beginning to like the idea. And I was convinced it was perfect.

But I didn't want to push it. "Well," I said, watching the sun set, "at least it's something to think about."

CHAPTER 6

Kristy

Tuesday

Dear Stacey,

Remember how great I said practice was going? Well, forget it. Now it stinks.

Everybody's dropping out! It is so frustrating! I don't even know if I'll have enough team members to play the Bashers!

And I will not forfeit the game to Bart Taylor. NO WAY, JOSÉ.

Even if I have to recruit Boo-Boo to play.

Details later. Miss you.

Kristy the Krushed Krusher

Boo-Boo is Watson's cat. I was not being serious.

But I thought about it.

Boy, was I steaming. I mean, we had been practicing two or three times a week. Everybody was excited about the game with the Bashers. The team was looking great.

Then, a couple of weeks ago, I received this postcard from Hannie Papadakis, saying she and Linny had to drop out. Okay. At full strength, we have twenty players. But we had lost five of them — Nicky, Claire, Margo, Buddy, and Suzi — to Sea City. Hannie and Linny made seven.

So as of the weekend, there were still thirteen players left for Friday's showdown. You only need nine to play, so we were in fine shape.

Or so I thought.

Saturday the Gianellis called from their summer house in the Berkshires. Mrs. Gianelli was going to stay there all week, selling real estate. Bobby and Alicia were having such a great time, they wanted to stay with her. Bobby is the newest member of our team.

Twelve players.

On Sunday I saw Haley Braddock. She reminded me of something I'd forgotten. Her brother Matt was leaving the next day for his special camp for the hearing impaired (he's been deaf since birth). Matt is our best hitter.

Eleven.

Then, on Monday, Mrs. Rodowsky called. Jackie had scratched his eye with a plastic drinking straw. Nothing too serious, but he had to wear a patch and would be very sensitive to light for a few days. He *might* be able to play on Friday, but he'd still have to wear the patch. On the left side. Jackie's a righty, so *left* is the side that faces the pitcher when the ball comes.

Now, I don't mean to be cruel to Jackie. I really do love him. But wherever he goes, an accident seems to follow. His nickname is "the Walking Disaster" — and that's with two normal eyes. I couldn't *imagine* what he'd be like with one eye.

Ten.

Still a team, with one to spare.

These were the brave souls who had stuck it out: the Kuhn kids, Jake (eight), Laurel (six), and Patsy (five); Myriah Perkins and her sister Gabbie (five and two and a half); Jamie Newton and Nina Marshall (both four); my brother David Michael (seven); and my stepsiblings, Karen (seven) and Andrew (four).

All ten showed up at our Tuesday practice at Stoneybrook Elementary School. (SES has been really nice about letting us use their play-ground all year.) As usual, some of the parents decided to stick around. As they climbed into the stands, I called out, "Okay, Krushers, who are we going to beat on Friday?"

"The Bashers!" they screamed.

"Who?" I said.

"The Bashers!"

"All *right*! That's more like it. Now let's have hitting practice!"

Jake Kuhn looked confused. "Shouldn't we wait for the others?"

"There are no others," I said. I explained what had happened, and said, "See, it's on our shoulders now."

"Oh," Jake muttered. Now he seemed worried and nervous. He looked into the stands, where his mom was sitting.

Jake's a little overweight, and he's self-conscious about it. It's not unusual for him to have an anxiety attack. I guessed I was putting too much pressure on him. "Don't worry, you'll do great," I reassured him.

"How can we play a practice game with only ten people?" David Michael asked. "That's only five on a side."

"We won't," I said. "We'll hit and catch and field, and then we'll play Round Robin."

Round Robin is another idea of mine. Nine players take the field and one goes to bat. Everyone else sits on the bench. If the batter gets a hit, he or she runs the bases as far as possible. Then, when the play is dead, everybody rotates. The batter becomes the right fielder, the right fielder becomes the center fielder, and so on. The pitcher goes to the bench and a new player gets to bat.

(Okay, you non-jocks can stop yawning now. I'm done.)

Anyway, the practice went pretty well. We had a few problems, though. In Round Robin, Nina Marshall hit the ball so far she went around the bases twice. I had to convince her that you can't score two runs in one turn at bat. Gabbie Perkins, who's so little that we have to use special rules (like pitching her a Wiffle ball instead of a softball), got bonked on the head on a slow chopper to second base, but she was all right.

I couldn't help but notice that Jake wasn't his old self. It wasn't until practice ended that I found out why.

As I packed up, I could see him whining about something to his mom. I minded my own business until I heard him say, "Can't we at least go on *Saturday*?"

"Jake, you know what the weekend traffic is like," his mom replied. "I'm taking a day off from work especially to do this . . ."

Uh-oh.

I saw Laurel and Patsy playing catch by the

first-base line. Casually I approached them and asked, "Um, when are you going on vacation?"

"This weekend," Laurel answered.

"Which day are you leaving?"

They looked at me blankly. Then they looked at each other. Then they shrugged.

"Mommy?" Patsy finally yelled. "What day are we leaving for Nantucket?"

"Friday morning," Mrs. Kuhn called back.

"Noooo!" Jake insisted, stomping his feet.

But Mrs. Kuhn had *Yes* in her eyes.

And I had to subtract three from ten.

We were sunk.

As I packed our stuff, I thought furiously. I had to find a solution to this. Who could I recruit? Which of our charges had shown any interest in sports? What about kids I'd never sat for?

A voice interrupted my thoughts. The last voice I wanted to hear.

"Hey, you guys getting ready to be bashed?"

Bart Taylor was walking toward the field, grinning.

Okay, I said I would tell you about Bart. Here are the most important things to know: He is seriously cute. He has deep brown eyes. His smile is a little crooked, and his hair looks naturally as if he just stepped out of a stylist's.

He's athletic, too, and he has a fantastic sense of humor.

All right, he's perfect. Well, almost. He can be really competitive — but then again, so am I. Anyway, he's the only guy I've ever *liked*.

And . . . he likes me!

I'm amazed that we stay friends, when I think about it. The Bashers are the only team we play, and they're older and bigger then we are. But the Krushers have beaten them, so our rivalry is *intense*.

And until Tuesday, I was sure we'd beat them again.

"Can I walk home with you guys?" he asked.

"Sure." I gathered my siblings together, and the four of us headed toward my house.

When I told Bart about our player shortage, he became very serious. "That's too bad," he said. "It really feels lousy to forfeit a game. When I was — "

I stopped walking. "What?"

"We had to forfeit once when I was in T-ball. Our coach came down with — "

"What do you mean, *forfeit*?" I snapped.

Bart shrugged. "Well, you can't play with only seven kids on your team, and if you can't play — "

"I'll have a full team by Friday," I said firmly.

"How?"

I looked him straight in the eye. Kristy Thomas was not going down without a fight. "Just watch."

In my old neighborhood, where Claudia lives, the houses are close together. Everyone knows each other.

Now I live in a neighborhood full of "top-out-of-sights." That's what Watson calls the people around us, because you can't see some of the houses from the road (they're at the ends of long driveways that wind uphill). Many of the kids go to private school or boarding school. So there were quite a few I'd never met.

But most of them were home for the summer. And that evening, I went after them.

With bat, ball, and clipboard in hand.

First I climbed one of the driveways to a modern-looking, wooden house.

DING-DING-DING-DONG-DI-DING-DING-DONNNNG!!

Brother. The doorbell played a symphony. That would drive me crazy.

I heard rumbling footsteps. The door opened. I expected to see someone like Lurch from the Addams family.

Yea! It was a kid. I figured he was about seven.

"Hi, I'm a neighbor of yours, Kristy Thomas. Do you like playing softball?"

The boy squinted at me. Then he turned and shouted, "Ma! Collection for Little Lea — "

"No!" I interrupted. I explained about the Krushers and asked if he were interested.

"But I'm in Challengers," he said.

"What?"

"You know, they pick you up on Saturdays and take you to the playing field in Stamford?"

I figured Challengers was some kind of fancy Little League for "top-out-of-sighters."

"Well, I'm offering you the chance to hone your skills *before* Saturday, with a real live championship game. Now, what's your name?"

"Phil Fields, but — "

I wrote his name down. When I looked up, a woman was standing at the door, holding out a five-dollar bill. "Here you go, dear," she said. "And good luck with the season."

It took forever to explain about the Krushers. When I left, Phil and his mom were giving me a weird look.

I went to the next house, which *was* visible

from the road. The youngest person there was about eighty-five.

I finally found another kid two houses away. Her name was Kate Munson, and she was mortified at my suggestion.

"But I — I don't know how to play," she stammered.

I smiled. "Nobody else does either! See, you're *perfect* for the team."

"But then how can you have a game if — ?"

"Well, I mean, they *didn't* know how, until I showed them how easy it is. Here, hold this bat."

I gave Kate a lesson. Right there on her doorstep. She was awful. Swinging the bat made her scared, so she'd let go, sending it through the air. I thought she was going to break her basement window.

But I could tell she liked playing. I wrote down her name and number.

Then there was S. Emerson Pinckney IV, "Quad" for short (don't ask me why). He probably weighed as much as half my team. And he came to the door with a Nintendo joystick in his hand. I tried my hardest, but it was a lost case. He did have a younger brother, though, who seemed to hang on to my every word. His name was "Moon" (short for P. Archibald). He was also . . . well, moon-shaped.

Next was Sheila Nofziger. You could have fit four of her into one Quad. She could barely lift the bat, but she was the most excited of all.

I went on until dark. In the end, I thought I could count on about six people — Kate, Moon, Sheila, and three others named Richard Owen, Kyle Abou-Sabh, and Alexandra DeLonge.

None of them had ever played softball. But they were going to learn.

And they were going to play on Friday, or my name wasn't Kristy Thomas.

MARGO

WENDSDAY

DEAR CAROLYN,
    GEUSS WHAT I FOUND TODAY? A TIDDAL
POOL! I CALLED IT A BEACH ZOO. THERE
WERE SO MANY CRETURES IN IT LIKE CRABS
AND CLAMES AND TENY FISHES IT WAS A
GRAT OPPURTUNTY FOR PEOPLE TO LERN
ABOUT MAUREEN LIFE. NOW ITS SUPPER. IM
ABOUT TO EAT A HOTDOG AND SOME COLD
SLAW AND THEN WATSH IT DOWN WITH SALTWATER.
JUST KIDDING !!!!!! BY !!!!!!
                    LOVE ALWAYS FOREVER.
                    MARGO THE ZOO KEEPER

I love the beach so much.

One of my favorite things is taking long walks. You can see the best sand castles that way. Sometimes you can watch seagulls swooping down into the water and coming up with fish. You can also see them swooping down into garbage cans and coming up with garbage, but that's disgusting.

In Sea City I saw all kinds of cool creatures. One time I found something that looked like a Baggie filled with water. I stooped to pick it up, but Mal was with me and she shouted, "Don't!"

It turned out it was a *poisonous* jellyfish. Ew! Ew!

I saw lots of clams. I didn't even know that the gross stuff inside it is actually its body. I saw one open and close. And I saw a kind that actually *spit* water. One time, Mal and I walked out on a jetty, and we saw blowfish swimming in the water. They looked like balloons, but Mal said they could be poisonous.

On Wednesday, Jessi, Claire, and I took the best nature walk. We were catching sand crabs in a bucket (we always let them go), and I noticed these tiny birds. After a wave came, they would follow the edge of the water back to the ocean. They'd peck-peck-peck with their beaks. Then, when the next wave came, they'd run away!

"What are those?" I asked Jessi.

"Sandpipers, I think," she said.

"Why do they go back and forth like that," I asked, "if they're so afraid of the water?"

Jessi shrugged. "I don't know. Maybe they pick up little bits of algae from the water as it washes back."

I asked Mom later on and she said Jessi was right. Jessi is so smart.

"What's algae?" Claire asked.

"Tiny little plants you can't see," Jessi replied.

"*I* can see them!" Claire insisted. She ran to the water, just like the sandpipers. She crouched low to look for algae. And she ran away when the sandpipers ran.

"Aaaaaaah!"

Claire was not a sandpiper. The wave crashed around her legs and she got scared. She stopped looking for algae.

Farther along, just past a jetty, the beach changed. The sand formed a cliff near the water. The waves would crash, then roll *juuust* up to the cliff. Every few feet there were these pools. Some were tiny but some were the size of a small car.

"Ooh, tidal pools!" Jessi said.

"Look!" I cried. One of the pools had creatures in it!

We ran to it. Claire screamed.

In the center of the pool was this huge, ugly crab. It looked like a helmet with a tail.

"That's a horseshoe crab," Jessi said.

"Is it dangerous?" Claire asked.

Jessi nodded. "I think so. If you step on one."

Claire and I crouched down to look, but we stayed pretty far back.

The pool was amazing. Around the horseshoe crab were a starfish, some snails, sand crabs, and a school of teeny black fish.

"Wow!" Claire said.

The starfish wiggled a little. That made the sand crab crawl sideways. The fish swam back and forth. The snails just sat there.

Then the horseshoe crab moved.

We ran away. But when we looked back, we could see it had barely gone anywhere. I guess it didn't really want to leave the water.

"Horseshoe crab-silly-billy-goo-goo!" Claire yelled.

Jessi and I burst out laughing.

"This is soooooo cool," I said. "They're all trapped. The water's like a cage, because the fish can't escape. If they did, they would dry up and die."

"Mm-hm," Jessi agreed.

"It's like a zoo," I went on. "A *beach* zoo."

"Yeah!" Claire said.

A beach zoo. What a great idea.

"I want everybody to see my beach zoo," I said. "We could put up a sign and charge admission."

"Admission?" Jessi looked at me as if I were crazy.

"Yeah. Come on!"

I ran all the way home. In the living room I found an empty cardboard box we'd packed stuff in. "Can I use this?" I called out.

Dad stuck his head out of the kitchen. "Sure. What are you going to do with it?"

"Make a sign."

I ripped off one side of the box (with Dad's help). Then I ran to my room and found a black marker and some tape.

In no time I had finished my sign. It looked like this:

COME TO MARGO'S!
SPECTAKTULER!!
BEACH ZOO!!!
SEE EXCOTIC AND DANGERUS SPESHIS OF
MAUREEN LIFE !!!!!
ONLY $50 CENTS

My dad came in and looked over my shoulder. "What's a beach zoo?"

I told him, and he said, "I'll get your mom."

I hurried outside. On the porch was a green shovel with a long handle. It was perfect. I carefully taped the sign to it, using *lots* of tape.

I could see Jessi and Claire by the water, with my brothers and sisters and the Barretts. I marched down there, holding my sign high. "Everybody come to the beach zoo!" I shouted.

"Beach zoo! Beach zoo! Silly-billy-goo-goo!" Claire shouted.

Jordan groaned. "You sound like Va*ness*a!"

Vanessa was building a sand castle with Buddy. She picked up a gloopy handful of wet sand and ran after Jordan.

Adam, Byron, Suzi, Jessi, and Mal followed me. Stacey promised she'd come later, after Buddy finished his castle.

When we reached the tidal pool, I stuck the shovel in the sand. My sign was standing straight up.

"Cool!" Adam said, crouching to see the horseshoe crab.

I stood in front of the zoo and held out my hand. "Only fifty cents for the experience of a lifetime."

"What?" Adam stood up and made a face. "Why should I pay *you*? I can see this for free! This is a public beach!"

"Adam . . ." Mal warned.

"Well, it's true, right, Byron?" Adam said.

"Yeah," Byron replied, trying to peer around me.

Adam turned away. "Let's go."

Byron followed him, then Suzi.

"Sorry, Margo," Mallory said.

"Tell the others the zoo is open," I said.

"Okay."

Jessi was the only one who stayed with me. I stood on the cliff. "Come to Margo's Beach Zoo!" I announced. "Only fifty cents."

Some people on blankets looked over but didn't get up.

A gray-haired couple walked by and peeked over the cliff. They just smiled and kept walking.

Some stupid kid ran by and tried to *step* in the beach zoo, but Jessi chased him away. She should have let him get bitten by the horse-shoe crab.

Soon Mom and Dad arrived with Mrs. Barrett. They each paid their admission fee — and they *loved* the zoo! Dad even turned the horse-shoe crab over. It was gross, with all these claws around a small hole (Dad said it was its mouth).

I stayed there the rest of the afternoon. I noticed the waves starting to come closer and closer to the pool.

Then Jessi and I saw a family set their blanket down. They had three kids. I told them about the zoo and they *all* came to see it!

Their oldest boy, George, reached the cliff first. He looked over and asked, "Where is it?"

"Right th — " I began.

But the waves were crashing against the edge of the cliff. The starfish, the snails, the sand crabs, and the fish were all gone.

As the waves went back, we could see the horseshoe crab. It was slowly trying to crawl to the water.

My sign was floating beside it.

The three kids ran after the horseshoe crab. I looked at Jessi. We shrugged. "That's why it's called a tidal pool," Jessi said. "The tide comes in."

I reached into my pocket. I had a dollar fifty.

Oh, well. If it weren't for the dumb tide, I know my zoo would have done really, really well. I could have been a millionaire.

CHAPTER 8

Jessi

Thursday

Dear Becca,

Every day there's
a new adventure down
here. Now it's building
sand castles! That's
all anyone wants to
do. There's going to
be a big contest next
week. And from what
I've seen, Sea City
must be the Official
Olympic City of Sand
Castles.

Give Squirt a kiss
and a long tickle
from me!

Love,
Jessi

"Ice creeeeeam . . ."
"Ice creeeeeam . . ."
"Ice creeeeeam . . ."
"Ice creeeeeam . . ."

Four guys wearing white aprons were singing in front of Ice-Cream Palace. They were probably high school age, maybe college. I guess they were supposed to be a barbershop quartet. The last guy who sang "Ice cream" had a voice like a high squawk. His neck veins stood out and his face turned bright red. He looked ready to explode.

But the singers were really good.

Claire, Margo, and Suzi stood in front of them with their mouths hanging open. If I didn't know them better, I'd think they'd forgotten about their ice cream.

It had taken us awhile to get to Ice-Cream Palace. The Sea City main drag is full of distractions. In fact, it's like one *long* distraction. There are souvenir shops, candy stores, a miniature golf course, and a place for every bad-for-you food imaginable. Like these:

Kotton Kandy Korner (why kan't they just spell the words korrectly?)

Hercules' Hot Dogs

Taffy 'n' Things

Burger Garden

Pizza Falafel (I think they mean pizza *and* falafel)

And my personal favorite, Chili Fotorama (do they put your snapshots *in* the chili or on the side?)

Of course, we had walked into almost every one of those places on the way to Ice-Cream Palace. But the Pikes and Mrs. Barrett had given me just enough money for cones. That was a wise idea, but it didn't make the trip easy for me.

I was constantly saying things like, "Are you *sure* you want taffy instead of ice cream?"

Anyway, the barbershop quartet finally reached the end of the song. For a flourish they reached into their apron pockets, took out metal ice cream scoops, thrust them in the air and shouted (what else?) "Ice Cream!"

A big crowd had gathered. We all applauded. The guys bowed and ran inside — and we all went in after them.

The four singers scurried behind the counter, ready to serve customers. The one with the deepest voice was very cute. He also happened to be an African-American, which didn't hurt. "Hi," he said. "Can I help you?"

"I want Rocky Road!" Margo blurted out.

"Pistachio Mustachio!" Claire shouted with a giggle.

"Chorcolate!" Suzi said.

"*Chor*colate?" I repeated.

Suzi smiled. "That's how Goofy says it!"

"How many scoops?" the cute guy asked.

"Two!" (Suzi.)

"Four!" (Margo.)

"Seven!" (Claire.)

"Whoa, I only have enough for one scoop for each of you," I said.

Triple moans and groans.

"Don't worry, I give big scoops," the guy said.

He was right. The kids walked out with little mountains of ice cream. (I had ordered a vanilla frozen yogurt. I was determined not to feel like a blimp when I returned to ballet class after vacation.)

On the way home, we passed by Pizza Falafel. On its counter, which faced the boardwalk, someone was buying a falafel plate. It looked like fried meatballs covered with a yummy-smelling sauce. "What's that?" Margo asked the counter man.

"Fried mashed chickpeas!" the man answered cheerfully.

The girls hurried away.

"Ooh, can we play miniature golf?" Suzi asked.

"Too *hard!*" Claire said. (According to Mal, Claire practically set a record for the most strokes per hole at Fred's Putt Putt.)

"Oooh, can we go in one of those?" Margo pointed to a small, wheeled, wicker carriage that was being pushed by a muscular guy. An elderly couple was sitting on the seat.

"Uh, maybe another time," I replied, imagining the puddles of ice cream between the wicker strands.

"Look! Look! Come here!" Now Suzi had plastered her face to a souvenir shop window. In it was a smiling, stuffed toy seagull, wearing a bib that said SEA CITY.

"Aw, he's *cute!*" cried Margo.

(He wasn't.) "Um, I don't have enough to — "

"I just want to *look*. Please please please please!"

"Oh, okay."

The girls stormed into the store. Suzi ran to the seagull and hugged it. She called it Scuttle, after the seagull in *The Little Mermaid*. Claire was fingering the chocolate bars at the candy counter, and Margo had her eye on one of those little snow globes.

The saleswoman was very nice. She gave each of the girls a pencil with Sea City stamped on it — for free.

The girls were ecstatic. I felt guilty because we weren't going to spend money there.

On the way out, I glanced at a big bulletin board outside the store. I saw a sign advertising a traveling circus on Sunday. When I read that aloud, the kids were determined to go. But another sign was even more interesting:

FIRST ANNUAL
SEA CITY
SAND CASTLE
CONTEST!

Wednesday afternoon, west of the jetty
Anyone may enter
Prizes in ALL categories!

"Yea!" Suzi screamed. "Let's all enter!"

"We're *great* at building castles!" Claire said.

You should have seen the girls. They jumped around so much I thought they'd lose what was left of their cones.

"Okay, when do you want to start practicing?" I asked.

"*NOW!*"

It was unanimous. The girls scarfed down their cones and ran toward the water.

In minutes I was helping them build castles. They were good, too. Suzi was especially skilled with wet sand. She could take a fistful and let it ooze out, making weird, goopy shapes.

We worked for a long time. We built a moat, a drawbridge, and a lookout tower. Claire tried

89

to make a troll under the drawbridge, but it looked more like a stalagmite.

As we were finishing up, Mal came over with the triplets, who were tossing a football around. Jordan was sucking on the last part of a Fudgsicle. "Hey, pretty good," he said when he saw our castle.

"We're going to win the sand castle contest," Margo announced proudly.

I thought Jordan was going to choke on his Fudgsicle. "What? You think you're going to enter the sand castle contest?"

"We don't *think*," Margo snapped.

"I know you don't," Jordan said.

Margo stuck out her tongue. I stood up and took Jordan aside. "Come on, Jordan — " I began.

"Have you seen the other castles?" Jordan asked.

"What other castles?"

"Down there." He pointed toward the jetty. I could see people doing *something* in the sand. "Come on, I'll show you."

Mal agreed to keep an eye on the girls. Jordan and I walked toward the jetty.

As we got closer, my jaw dropped open. The people I'd seen were building castles.

Castles? These were medieval villages — kingdoms! I half expected horses to come out of them.

The builders were mostly grown-ups, and they were working in teams. They were using fancy molds and carving tools. One group was even using sand bricks! The detail was amazing — plastic windows and doors, wooden drawbridges that *worked*, real pennants flying from the towers, different-colored sand (is there such thing as *sand dye*?).

"Oh, boy . . ." I murmured.

"I told you," Jordan said.

The girls' castle was nothing compared to these. But I didn't want to insult them by saying they shouldn't enter.

So far, my week had been great. I'd been a perfect mother's helper, just like I wanted to be. But this was going to be trouble. Feelings were going to be hurt.

I had no idea what to do.

CHAPTER 9

Mary Anne

Friday

Dear Mallory,
    We did it! We
actually had our
mini-camp sleepover!
And boy, was it a
night to remember.
We camped out, played
games, and told
stories. And... we may
have had a visit from
a ghost!
                    Love
                    Mary Anne

P.S. Don't be scared. The
ghost part isn't true
(I don't think).

I don't know how Dawn convinced me to hold an outdoor sleepover.

I'm not the type of person who likes to camp out. I prefer a nice, soft bed with a roof over my head and an air conditioner.

Anyway, we decided to hold it on Thursday night, the night before the last day of Mini-Camp. It would be in the barn if it rained, outside if the weather was nice. We called all the parents and got permission. Everybody loved the idea except the Prezziosos. They didn't think it was appropriate for their angel to be roughing it. But they changed their minds when Jenny threw a tantrum.

Thursday evening was cloudy. Dawn and I prepared for an outdoor campout. hoping it wouldn't rain. We had bought marshmallows, graham crackers, and chocolate bars for s'mores. (We had had a barbecue for dinner, so Dad and Sharon said we could use the glowing coals.) We set out several huge blankets, then rolled out sleeping bags for Marilyn and Carolyn, who didn't have them.

Jenny was the first to arrive. Her dad brought her over. She was wearing pink slippers and pj's with unicorns on them. She was also clutching a ragged red doll that had been patched a million times.

"She won't go to sleep without it," Mr.

Prezzioso said in an apologetic voice. He set down the fluffiest, most expensive-looking kid's sleeping bag I had ever seen. Rolled up with it was a foam rubber pad. "She likes a soft sleeping surface."

Marilyn and Carolyn, who couldn't come to the Stones' farm, came next. Then the Hobart brothers, then Charlotte. Myriah and Jamie arrived last.

Were they adorable! Mathew and Johnny wore short-shorts pj's, but Jamie had Doctor Dentons on. "So my feet won't get dirty if I have to get up during the night," he explained.

After the parents left, the kids rolled out their sleeping bags on the blankets. Charlotte began to look awfully worried about something. "Um, Dawn?" she asked. "What happens if we . . . you know, if we have to . . ."

"Go pee-pee!" Johnny announced.

"You can use the bathroom in the house," Dawn said. "Or . . . go outside, if you want."

That made the campers explode with giggles.

"Who wants to play games?" I asked.

"ME!"

Our yard is perfect for running around, so we played Red Light, Green Light; Freeze Tag; and some other games, until it got too dark to see.

Then it was time for s'mores!

We sat around the grill. By that time the coals were almost dead, but they did soften the marshmallows a little. Dawn had brought out some sesame sticks for herself (*un*toasted, of course) — and *those* caught on, too. She had to run inside and get a whole bagful.

Things were going just great, until I began hearing a *psssss . . . psssss* noise.

Mathew heard it, too. "What's that?"

"Maybe it's a ghost," Jenny said.

Jamie's eyes bugged open. "Um, I want to go home."

Pssss . . .

Then I felt something. A drop. It was starting to rain. "You know what that noise is?" I said. "Raindrops hitting the coals. I hate to say it, but we have to move this campout inside the barn."

"Then it's a camp*in*, not a campout," Carolyn said.

We scooped up the sleeping bags and dragged them to the barn. I turned on the light. "Spread them out on the hay," I suggested.

After we set up again, I could see some yawning faces. And some sad ones. Like Jamie's.

"What's up?" I said, kneeling beside him.

"I — I just . . . I mimamandadee," he mumbled.

"You what?"

In the teeniest voice, he said, "I miss my mommy and daddy."

I put my arm around him. "I know how you feel. And you don't have to stay if you don't want to. I thought we'd tell a few bedtime stories, and then if you still want to go, my dad can take you home."

I could see a flicker of interest in Jamie's eyes when I mentioned bedtime stories. "Can you tell a scary one?" he asked.

"You *want* a scary story?"

He nodded. "With monsters!"

"Dragons!" Mathew added.

"Worms!" Johnny shouted.

"Worms?" Jenny repeated. "That's dumb."

"No, giant, slimy blood-sucking ones!" Johnny said.

Jenny made a face. "Ew."

"How about a ghost story?" Charlotte asked.

"Great idea!" Dawn said. "In fact, there may be a ghost, right on this property."

Charlotte smiled and settled into a pile of hay. Jamie, Myriah, and Johnny stared at Dawn, wide-eyed. Carolyn and Mathew looked skeptical. Marilyn giggled and said, "Get out of here."

"It's true," Dawn said. "Or at least some people think it is. You see, almost two hundred years ago, this house belonged to the Mullray family. But they ran into some trouble, and Old Man Mullray had to move the family to Vermont. Well, two of his children went, but his youngest son, Jared, refused to leave. On the morning of the move, when the bank officials came to claim the property, Old Man Mullray called for his son, and they all heard Jared answer, 'I ain't leaving!'

"But the voice wasn't coming from the house, or the barn. It seemed to be coming from someplace in between. No one ever found Jared Mullray, and to this day, some people think he's still rattling around."

"R-r-really?" Jamie asked.

"I heard that story before," Jenny said.

"Ah, but you never heard of Priscilla Gatlin, Jared's fiancee," Dawn said.

Jenny shook her head. The kids leaned forward.

I gave Dawn a Look (*I* had never heard of Priscilla Gatlin).

"Priscilla was madly in love with Jared. But her father was a common blacksmith whose business had fallen on hard times. Old Man Mullray wouldn't hear of the marriage. He figured a move to Vermont would solve his son's crush on this unworthy girl.

"After the old man moved away, Priscilla would visit the farm. She would just sit

97

on the porch, always waiting. Waiting and hoping that Jared would come for her.

"But months went by and he never did. Soon another man in town, Obadiah Spooner, took a liking to Priscilla. One day he followed her when she came to this house. He sat on the porch and said the sweetest things to her. But Priscilla had her heart set on Jared and no one else.

"Then one day it happened. Jared came back. Or at least his voice did.

"Priscilla was sitting on the porch with Obadiah again. This time Obadiah was asking for her hand in marriage. And poor Priscilla, even though she still loved Jared, was tempted to say yes. Obadiah was a wealthy man, and although he had a wart in the middle of his nose, he was kind. Every time he visited Priscilla, he made sure his black hair was brushed handsomely.

"Before Priscilla could answer Obadiah, a muffled voice called, 'Come to the barn . . . come to the barn . . .'

"Well, Priscilla sat straight up. She forgot about Obadiah. The voice belonged to her beloved Jared! She raced to the barn — *this* barn. She flung open the door — "

Dawn fell silent.

"What happened?" Myriah said, her voice a squeak.

100

Dawn took a deep breath. "The barn was pitch-black. Obadiah called after her, 'Priscilla, stop! No!' But there was no keeping her from her true love. Priscilla walked in.

"Then there was a scream — followed by silence. Obadiah took out his gun and ran into the barn. Shots were fired, *Bang! Bang!*

"Neighbors came running. No one was foolish enough to go inside, so they waited . . . and waited . . ."

"Then what?" Jamie asked.

"Only one person came out. It was a man with hair as white as snow, sticking straight into the air. His eyes were wide open and glassy, as if he'd seen something no man was supposed to see. No one recognized him until he came closer. Then they could see the wart on the nose."

"Obadiah!" Charlotte said.

"Yes. He noticed no one as he walked out. He went straight to his house, lay down on his bed and never again got up, although he lived a good twenty years more. The neighbors went into the barn then, but no one else was inside. Not Priscilla, not Jared. Not a trace. Some say Jared was alive, and took her to Alaska to marry him. Others say the ghost killed Priscilla. Still others say that Priscilla, too, became a ghost, and to this day she walks the barn, looking for Jared."

The only sound in the barn was the tapping of rain on the roof. The kids were open-mouthed. I could see Dawn reaching toward the trap door (there actually is a secret passageway that leads from the barn to the house). But I gave her a sharp Look. If she opened that door, no one would sleep that night.

Including me.

Just to be safe, I stood up and rolled a lawn mower onto the trap door.

"I think they're both still alive," Carolyn whispered.

"If they went to Alaska, maybe they turned into Santa and Mrs. Claus," Johnny said.

Charlotte yawned. So did I. "Listen, guys, it's getting late now. What do you say — " I was going to suggest lights out, but that didn't seem like such a great idea. " — we go to sleep?"

There weren't any protests. One by one, everyone began to nod off. "Good job," I whispered to Dawn. "Where'd you hear that?"

She shrugged. "I made it up."

"Fantastic!"

I put my head down. It *was* a good story — and a good sleepover. But I had a hard time falling asleep.

I couldn't keep my eyes off the lawn mower.

CHAPTER 10

Claudia

Friday

Dear Stacey,
    Im about to leave for my last day
of sumer school. I cant balieve I
actualy feel sad. (just a little) Wierd,
huh? The kids turned out to be prety
nice. Oh well, by the time this card
gets to you, I will be in Sea City! And
I will read it and probly wonder
how I coud have felt anything but
extatic!   Can't Wait!!!! (really.)
                                Claud

103

"Good morning, class."

It had been twenty long, long days. And old Mrs. Wegmann had begun each one with the same highly original greeting. For twenty days, the fluorescent light above the left side of the room had given off the same annoying buzz. For twenty days, I had been counting backward from twenty.

Now I was at One. At long last, the Summer of Torture was ending.

I should have been thrilled. Thrilled? I should have been dancing on my desk. I'd gotten decent grades. Good enough so that I was guaranteed to pass even if I flunked the final exam. All I had to do was sit there and not commit a crime. When the bell rang, I would be ready for G-M-O-O-H:

Get Me Out Of Here!

And then I could start thinking about serious things. Like which bikinis to take to Sea City.

"Well, here we are, our last day," Mrs. Wegmann droned on. (Duh, no kidding.) "I'll give you some time for questions, then we'll have our final exam."

You know what? Four kids asked questions, and I knew the answers to each one! Me, Claudia "The Smart One" Kishi, budding math genius!

The test began. There were a few tough problems, but mostly they weren't too bad. I even managed to finish a little early, believe it or not.

While I was waiting for the official end, I looked around the class (not too obviously, so Mrs. Wegmann wouldn't think I was cheating).

Carly's tongue was hanging out of her mouth—and she was *chewing* on it. *Very* suave. I wanted to giggle and tell her.

I looked at the clock. Two minutes till the end of summer school. Feelings began rising up inside me. Half of me wanted to celebrate, but the other half felt a little sad. I would miss my new friends.

Don't get me wrong. If I had had one more day of summer math — one more *hour* — I think I would have passed out.

But still . . .

BRRIIIINNNG!

"Class, have a wonderful rest of the summer!" Mrs. Wegmann shouted over the cheering.

We ran out of the room, throwing our papers on her desk. Out in the hallway, Carly practically started screaming. "We did it! We did it!"

Theresa shouted, "We are officially *not* stupid!"

We gave each other a big hug and danced around.

"Speak for yourself," grumbled another classmate, named Fran. "I think I'm going to have to repeat this stuff again."

"Oh, Fran, no you won't," Carly said. "You passed the quizzes, right?"

"Most of them," Fran answered.

"Okay, look," I said. "What answer did you get on the word problem about the doughnut bakery?"

As we discussed the test, Fran began feeling better. A lot of our answers were the same.

We walked together through the front door of the school. As we waited for the bus to arrive, we started feeling nostalgic.

"Remember the day Mrs. Wegmann had the hiccups?" Theresa asked.

"And the time David Gabel called her Mrs. Wigwam?" Carly piped up.

Another classmate, Barbara, grinned at me. "And that quiz you thought you'd brought your calculator to, but it was your VCR remote?"

We all howled.

"I'm going to miss you guys," Carly said sadly.

"Oh!" Theresa blurted. "What are you guys doing Sunday?"

Everyone said "Nothing," except me. I told

them about Sea City. Just *mentioning* it made me feel wonderful, until Theresa spoke up again: "Because my mom and dad said I could have an end-of-school barbecue for us."

"I can go," Carly said.

"Me too," Fran and Barbara added.

My heart sank. I really wanted to go to that party. But I was supposed to leave with Mrs. Barrett's boyfriend and his kids on Saturday. Maybe I could tell him I'd stay and take a bus on Monday —

Stay? Was I crazy? I'd only been looking forward to this for a whole summer!

A school bus roared up to the front door, which meant Barbara and Theresa had to leave.

" 'Bye, Claudia!" they said. "We'll miss you!"

"Me too!" I replied.

"Write, okay?" Barbara said.

"I will!"

We hugged, and promised to keep in touch. Theresa said she'd have another party at the beginning of school.

They climbed in. We kept shouting " 'Bye!" to each other through the open windows.

Carly, Fran, and I walked home. Fran's house was closest to the high school and mine

was next. At each one we had a long, tearful good-bye.

At home, I ran straight to my room to begin packing. I felt *much* less excited than I had expected. In fact, when Dawn and Mary Anne came by to visit, the first thing Mary Anne said was, "Are you okay?"

"Yeah, fine," I replied.

"Want to go to the Krushers game with us?" Dawn asked.

"It's actually happening?" I said.

Mary Anne nodded. "You know Kristy. She managed to put a team together."

"This I have to see." I pulled a suitcase out of my closet and opened it up.

Inside were three bags of pretzels. I'd forgotten all about them.

So . . . we snacked while we packed.

Mary Anne and Dawn told me about the famous Mini-Camp overnight. Mary Anne said she had awakened in the middle of the night to a noise.

"I could have sworn it was a female voice," she said, "calling out, 'Carrot! Carrot!' I thought Charlotte was calling for her dog in her sleep." (Carrot is the name of Charlotte's schnauzer.)

I shrugged. "Was she?"

"No," Mary Anne replied solemnly. "She was fast asleep. But I know who the voice belonged to. It was the ghost of Priscilla Gatlin, saying, *'Jared! Jared!'''*

"Oh, stop!" I could feel myself shivering.

Dawn laughed. "Mary Anne woke me up. Then she went back to sleep — and *I* couldn't sleep. Then Jamie woke up whining. I thought he was having a ghost dream, too, but he just had to go to the bathroom."

Our conversation turned to Sea City. We talked about the postcards we'd received. We gabbed away until I was all packed. By that time I was fully, totally, one hundred percent psyched about Sea City.

And I couldn't wait to see Kristy's new Krushers.

CHAPTER 11

Kristy

Friday

Hi, Sam!

How's camp? Do you like being a counselor? I hope you have a VCR there. If you do, go to the nearest town and rent _The Bad News Bears_.

Multiply that by ten. Then you'll have an idea of what the Krushers' championship game with the Bashers was like.

Your frazzled sister,

Kristy

"Come on, pitcher!" Kyle Abou-Sabh shouted. He cocked his bat, ready to smack a practice line drive.

"Kyle, that's first base," I said. "Home plate is to your left."

I gently pushed him in the right direction.

Moon Pinckney was already at home plate, taking some warm-up swings of his own. He seemed to be getting the hang of it — except for one minor thing.

"Uh, Moon," I said, "take your glove *off* when you bat."

"Oh," he replied.

As he removed his glove, I noticed something else. "And when you *do* wear it, it goes on your right hand, not your left."

"But I'm a lefty," he said.

"Exactly," I replied. "You'll be able to leave your left hand free to throw. Besides, look where the thumb is."

I left Moon staring at his mitt.

Kate Munson was playing catch with Myriah Perkins near the third-base line. Myriah was pitching very gently to her.

And Kate was ducking each throw as if it were a hand grenade.

Richard Owen had brought a tennis ball to the game and looked confused.

Alexandra DeLonge had come dressed in a

112

brand-new designer baseball outfit. She was trying desperately to wipe off a smudge of dust from her right ankle. In the stands, her parents and grandparents were having a champagne picnic and toasting each other.

Sheila Nofziger was picking dandelions in left field.

"Let's look alive, guys!" I shouted. "The Bashers will be coming any minute!"

Actually, the Bashers weren't due for another half hour, but we were in dire need of serious practice.

I had gotten a team together, all right. But what a team. Our only hope was that the Bashers would be laughing so hard they'd pass out and forfeit the game.

I'm exaggerating. I was much more optimistic than that. For one thing, we hadn't lost any more Krushers that week. We still had seven original members. If I kept them all in the game, that meant only two of my new people had to play at any one time. (Of course, I'd rotate them so they'd all have a chance to play.)

Alexandra wasn't a bad catcher. And I could put the other new player in right field, where he or she couldn't do much harm. (Why? Because most batters tend to hit to the opposite field: righties to left field and vice versa. So, since most batters are righties, not too many balls are hit to right field. That's a bit of Kristy Thomas Baseball Wisdom, and you heard it here, folks.)

When the Bashers did arrive, Bart stood by the batting cage and watched the end of our practice. I tried not to talk to him, but he tracked me down.

"Are you sure you don't want to cancel?" he asked.

"Not on your life," I said. "We're here, aren't we?"

"Kristy, look, you don't have to forfeit, okay? We can just drop the game — or postpone it."

I smiled and shook my head. "I'm not a quitter, Bart."

He took off his cap, looked out to the field, and scratched his head. "Okay. But, uh, maybe you should tell your outfielders to stop playing patty-cake."

Sure enough, Sheila and Kate were playing some hand-clapping game in centerfield. As Bart walked away, I ran to them and said it was time to play ball.

Sheila looked surprised. "Oh, darn!" she complained, skulking away.

Oh, darn? Why did she think we were all here?

The Bashers, being bigger and older, held a very short practice. A very short and *disciplined* practice. Honestly, I don't know why Bart ever organized this team. His players could join Little League or T-ball, no sweat.

Moon was staring at them, google-eyed. "W-we're playing *them*?" he whispered.

"Hey, we've beaten them before," I said in the most confident voice I could manage.

Then it was time to begin. The remaining BSC members had shown up. They were in the stands, cheering and looking, well, *dubious*.

Watson had agreed to be the home plate umpire. Even though Watson's obviously a Krushers fan, Bart hadn't protested a bit. (I guess he knew we needed all the help we could get.)

Bart and I met with Watson at the pitcher's mound. We agreed to play seven innings. Then Watson tossed a quarter and I won the toss. We would take the field first.

Our pitcher was Marilyn Arnold. Alexandra was behind the plate, catching. Kyle was in right field, looking lost. Another questionable player was at second base. David Michael was our shortstop, so I hoped he'd be able to handle anything hit to the infield.

The first Basher batter stepped up. He wore a confident smile. He took a few practice swings, so hard you could hear the wind swoosh.

Bart shouted, "Take it to right field!"

Now Kyle looked terrified.

I closed my eyes and prayed.

"Ball one!" Watson called out.

"New pitcher new pitcher new pitcher new pitcher!" one of the Bashers kept repeating.

"Knock it off!" David Michael yelled. "You're boring!"

"Ball two!" Watson barked.

"Come on, get it over the plate!" the batter taunted.

Marilyn walked him on four pitches. He sauntered to first base, spitting every few feet, as if he were a pro.

"Keep cool, Marilyn, looking good," I said. (Okay, I was lying.)

The next batter hit the ball between second and third. David Michael scooped it up. He turned to throw to second.

Our second baseperson was drawing a happy face in the dirt. "Look up!" David Michael screamed.

Too late.

The ball hit second base and bounced into right field.

Kyle froze. He pointed to himself, as if to say, "Me?"

"Throw it to third, Kyle!" I yelled.

Kyle squatted, waiting for the ball to come to him. It rolled between his legs. He bent

116

down to watch, like an ostrich just before it buries its head.

"Go get it!" I called out.

He ran after it, picked it up, and threw with all his might. Richard Owen made a perfect catch.

Unfortunately, Richard Owen was sitting on the bench.

Both batters were jumping on home plate. "Inside-the-park home run!" they squealed.

"Unh-uh," I protested. "Interference from the sidelines. That's a ground-rule double!"

"Ask the ump," Bart said calmly.

I looked at Watson. He smiled and shrugged. "Sorry, the runners crossed home before Richard touched the ball."

"Two to nothing!" the first batter gloated.

"You *guys*," Alexandra groaned. "Why don't you watch where you're going!"

She was standing behind home, dusting off her pants. The runners had kicked up a cloud of dirt around her.

"Can I call a time out, to change?" Alexandra asked Watson.

"Oh, brother . . ." I muttered to myself.

I closed my eyes and sat on the bench. This was going to be a long game.

The final score was 34–1, Bashers. Our one run came when Gabbie whacked her Wiffle ball

past the Bashers pitcher, who had moved in close. The third baseman picked up the ball and threw it so hard it sailed into the stands, and my older brother Charlie hid it.

Gabbie skipped around the bases and scored. Even the Bashers cheered her.

After the game, no one seemed particularly crushed. Some of my new players even seemed proud of themselves — which was great. I congratulated them on their play and complimented them to their parents.

Claudia, Dawn, Mary Anne, and Watson all tried to tell me what a phenomenal job I'd done.

Inside, however, I felt as if I'd just tried to move a boulder up a hill by blowing on it with a straw.

I was tired. But I was proud we hadn't given up.

Bart found me later and said, "Good game. Have fun in Sea City."

I think I answered him, but I don't remember what I said.

I walked home from the game with David Michael, Karen, and Andrew. Karen looked upset.

"It's okay," I told her. "We did the best we could, and we had fun."

"I know," she said. "It's just that . . . that . . . ."

"What?"

She sighed. "Well, Nannie and I baked a victory cake for you, Kristy. It was supposed to be a surprise. It says 'Congratulations, Coach,' on it — and we *lost*!"

"That's so sweet, Karen!" I said. "I don't care what it says. It's the thought that counts."

We walked on in silence. But just before we reached the house, Karen's face lit up. "See you!" she said, and she raced inside.

David Michael, Andrew, and I walked into a living room decorated with streamers and balloons. "Surprise!" Mom and Watson called out.

A few minutes later Nannie and Karen came in from the kitchen. Karen was proudly holding a cake. The icing looked smudged, but the letters were clear enough.

They said GOOD-BYE, COACH!

"We're going to miss you, Kristy," Karen said.

I had been so busy with the Krushers, I'd almost forgotten about Sea City. I was leaving the next day!

I suddenly felt much happier.

"Oh, thanks, you guys," I said. "I'll miss you, too."

My "victory" party? Well, it turned into the nicest farewell celebration I could imagine.

CHAPTER 12

Stacey

Saturday

Dear Charlotte,
     Well, the Baby-sitters Club is together once again. Yea! We had so much fun catching up. The weather was incredible today, too.
     But not for long. Guess what? We may be in the middle of a huge hurricane soon! And there's a lady nearby who looks like Miss Gulch— and she rides a bike. Wee-dee-dee-dee, wee-dee-dee-dee (Twilight Zone theme). At least we aren't going to have a tornado.
     See you in a week — if I'm not in the Emerald City!

                    Luv always,
          Your almost sister,
                    Stacey

"AAAAAAAAAGGGGGHHHHHH!"

No, that was not the cry of the Wicked Witch of the West as she melted.

It was the happy screaming of seven Baby-sitters Club members. (Well, there were eight of us, but Logan managed to keep his jubilation to a boyish smile.)

Claudia, Dawn, Kristy, Mary Anne, and Logan had arrived with Mrs. Barrett's boyfriend, Franklin Harris. He has four kids from a previous marriage: Lindsey (who's eight), Taylor (six), Madeleine (four), and Ryan (two).

Ten people in a van! No wonder they looked so happy to be out.

The conversation sounded like this:

"We had such a . . ."

" . . . feels so good . . ."

" . . . Mini-Camp . . ."

" . . . six new players . . ."

" . . . I missed you . . ."

" . . . me too . . ."

" . . . Rosebud . . ."

" . . . summer school . . ."

" . . . Elvira . . ."

" . . . you should have seen . . ."

Finally Kristy stuck her fingers in her mouth and let out a loud whistle. "Okay, let's get settled first! Then we can catch up!"

Once a president, always a president.

The Pikes had worked out sleeping arrangements with Mrs. Barrett. Dawn would stay at the Barretts' to take care of Franklin's kids. Logan, Kristy, Claudia, and Mary Anne would stay at the Pikes'. On Monday night, Logan would go back to Stoneybrook with Franklin and his gang (Logan had to work on Tuesday), and then Dawn would move to the Pikes'.

I wasn't thrilled about that last part. I kind of wished Mrs. Barrett would say, "Oh, the Pikes' house is so crowded. Surely Dawn can stay with us!"

Uh-uh, no way, didn't even think of it.

Well, that was understandable, I guess. After all, Dawn had been invited by the Pikes in the first place.

Dawn and I ran upstairs to my room. A trundle bed was there, and I had set it up for her.

"We're roommates!" Dawn squealed, plopping her suitcase on the bed.

"Yeah!" I squealed back.

Dawn pulled a bathing suit out of her suitcase and began to change. "Tell me everything, Stacey. Claudia told me you saw Toby. And he acted as if nothing had happened."

I sighed. "Yeah. What a dork. I just said, 'Hit the road, Jack. You're blocking my sunlight.' "

124

Dawn screamed. "No! You *didn't.*"

"You're right. I didn't. But I was really cold to him. And you know what that creep did? He started flirting with Mallory!"

"*Mallory?* No! Serious?"

"Serious. She and I haven't been talking much."

"Has he asked her out?"

"Oh my lord, no! She'd have told me *that*! Besides, he's not interested in her. She's eleven."

We gossiped for a few more minutes. I told her a little about how difficult Mrs. Barrett had been, but I didn't go into details. It was noon, and I'd promised Mrs. Barrett we'd take the kids to the beach.

We gathered up the kids and trooped next door to the Pikes'. Everybody was ready, and Kristy began lining us up in front of the porch as if we were in a race.

"Come on, take your positions," she ordered us.

"*Kristyyyy,*" Dawn said.

"On your marks . . ."

Dawn and I sighed. Buddy and his sisters thought this was a great idea. So did Franklin's kids.

"Get set. . . . GO!"

Kristy, Claudia, Mary Anne, Jessi, Mal, Nicky, Margo, Vanessa, Claire, Buddy, Suzi,

Marnie, Lindsey, Taylor, Madeleine, Ryan, Dawn, and I all began running. Sand flew everywhere. Our charges shrieked with joy. Then I shrieked. Then Dawn. Then everyone else — including Mary Anne.

Logan was already on the beach, playing Frisbee with the triplets. The boys stared at us as if we were a landing of alien invaders.

I didn't care. We were all here. It was the happiest I'd felt in a week!

In case we were wondering whether Kristy's Idea Power diminished outside of Stoneybrook, we found out that day.

It didn't.

Somehow Kristy had devised a way to convince the grown-ups to take the kids for a half hour. From five-thirty to six. Do you know why?

You guessed it. A Baby-sitters Club meeting!

Without phones, without records, without dues. The best kind.

We gathered in the Pikes' kitchen, still in our bathing suits. The wind was whipping in from the sea, through the screen door. We wrapped our towels around us.

Mal had decided to change before the meeting. When she entered the kitchen, she saw an empty chair between Jessi and me.

She decided to stand near the doorway. (Which, to be honest, was okay with me.)

A radio was droning on the windowsill. As we gabbed away, Kristy shushed us.

" . . . *low pressure system moving in tonight, the lows in the upper fifties. This is WCCT, Sea City. The time at the tone will be five-thirty. . . .*"

At the sound of the *beeeeep*, Kristy pounded her fist on the table. "I call this meeting to order!"

A plastic salt shaker clattered to the floor.

Claudia rolled her eyes. "Puh-leeze, Kristy."

"I hearby declare a special emergency gossip session of the Baby-sitters Club," Kristy went on.

We cheered.

"First, a report from the president regarding the Krushers' heartbreaking loss!"

Kristy told us every detail of her game. Then Claudia described her new summer school pals and cracked us up with an imitation of her teacher. Dawn and Mary Anne talked about Mini-Camp and the sleepover. Then us Sea Cityers told of our adventures down here.

I hadn't laughed so hard in a long, long time. We were *gasping*.

I couldn't help but notice that Logan didn't say much. He looked sort of tired. I thought he might have felt left out, so I asked, "How's your job, Logan? Do you still like it?"

He shrugged. "It's okay, I guess. Hard work, though."

That was it from the male camp. Oh, well. I figured he was too exhausted to say much. Or maybe the job was boring.

In the conversation's lull, we could hear the radio again:

" . . . *we have a report now that Tropical Storm Bill is picking up speed and moving northwest, about four hundred miles off the coast of Jamaica. It's too early to tell what will happen, but if it continues in its current path it could become the first major hurricane of the year . . ."*

"Wow," Jessi said. "I'm glad we're not in Jamaica."

I'd never been in a hurricane. I wondered if it was like a tornado. I started thinking about *The Wizard of Oz.*

Then Claudia remembered another funny story about summer school. Kristy turned the radio off, and we began laughing our heads off again.

CHAPTER 13

LOGAN

SATURDAY

HEY, KERRY AND HUNTER!

YOU GUYS HAVE TO SEE THIS PLACE. YOU WOULD LOVE IT. MARY ANNE AND I TOOK A WALK ON THE BOARDWALK TONIGHT. THERE'S EVERYTHING — INCLUDING THIS MONSTER FERRIS WHEEL AND MILES OF ARCADE GAMES.

I WISH I COULD STAY HERE MUCH LONGER. TOO BAD I HAVE TO GO BACK TO THE ROAD SPUD. OH, WELL, SEE YOU MONDAY, AND DON'T DRIVE MOM AND DAD CRAZY WHILE I'M GONE!

YOUR COMMANDER-IN-CHIEF,
GENERAL LOGAN

The Road Spud is my nickname for the Rosebud Cafe. Actually, I didn't make it up. It's kind of a busboy tradition to call it that. You can say it and no one realizes you're making fun of the name.

But enough of that. That's another story.

Anyway, there I was in Sea City. I was really happy to see Mary Anne. I was not happy to be the only male among the entire Baby-sitters Club for two whole days — but I could deal with that.

I mean, the BSC members are some of my best friends. They're nice and funny and smart. They're just not guys (duh, bet you didn't know that). Which means when I'm in a room with them, they sometimes feel they can't talk normally to each other.

Do you know what it's like to be surrounded by seven girls who love to yak but can't go all out? It's awkward. Awkward? I break into a sweat that feels like a monster slimed my shirt collar.

But to tell you the truth, things were pretty cool at Sea City. Everyone seemed relaxed in our impromptu kitchen meeting. There was hardly any giggling-with-hands-over-mouths or funny looks at me and Mary Anne.

I have to admit I was thinking of something else. Just slightly. You see, Mary Anne met this guy named Alex down here.

Now I don't want you to think I'm a raving jealous type. I'm really not. Besides, Mary Anne told me they were only friends, and I believe her. And Alex supposedly has a girlfriend back home. But I don't know. Sea City is a romantic spot, and Mary Anne and Alex went out to eat together and stuff, and just the idea that she and he were enjoying a vacation here while I was in Stoneybrook. . . .

Well, what can I say? I'm human. It bugged me.

But just a little.

After the BSC meeting, Mary Anne and I took a walk along the beach. It was cool outside, like fall, which meant Mary Anne snuggled up close to me, which I liked a lot.

"Logan, it feels so good to be here with *you*," she said.

"Yeah," I answered. "Do you miss being a mother's helper?"

She snuggled closer and smiled. "Not now."

We passed about fifty yards' worth of monster sand castle construction. I saw some incredibly complex stuff, but that work seemed like such a waste. I mean, it's *sand*. Sooner or later it all has to come down.

Just beyond the construction site was a jetty. Beyond that was a group of kids playing. Two guys, about our age, were taking care of them.

"Hi!" Mary Anne shouted.

The kids turned around. So did the two guys. They grinned when they saw us.

Mary Anne ran excitedly toward them. I followed, at a slower pace.

The kids excitedly showed Mary Anne their castles and holes.

When I reached them, Mary Anne said, "Logan, this is Toby and this is Alex."

"Hey, how's it going?" Toby said.

"What's up?" Alex asked. "Mary Anne told me all about you."

Both were still grinning. They stuck out their hands and I shook them.

So this was Alex.

He was pretty good-looking, I noticed. I wouldn't cast him in a teen heart-throb movie, but as looks go, his were solid.

Mary Anne took my arm and squeezed close to me.

"Pretty cool out tonight," I said.

(Well, I had to say something.)

"Brrrrrr," Mary Anne agreed, holding me tighter.

I got the feeling Mary Anne wanted to make *sure* Alex knew I was her boyfriend.

"Yeah," Alex said. "Well, just as long as we don't get hit by Bill."

It took me a minute to realize he meant the tropical storm.

We fell silent then, just kind of smiling and nodding and shifting weight. Then one of the kids called out, "Alex, look at my maze!"

"Well, nice meeting you!" Alex said. "Got to go!"

Everyone said good-bye. Mary Anne and I turned and walked back to the Pikes'.

And that was that. I think Mary Anne was nervous, but I felt fine. I mean, it was no big deal. There's no law that a guy's girlfriend must *never* have any male friends.

Anyway, I was bigger than him.

Alex was not mentioned the rest of the night. I made sure of it. I didn't want to blow up anything that really wasn't important.

Dinner at the Pikes' was a madhouse. We cooked up eight pounds of hamburger meat and twenty-seven hot dogs.

Afterward, Mary Anne and I had an actual date on the boardwalk. What a place! We took a long romantic stroll . . . until I saw bumper cars.

"We have to go on these!" I said.

So we did. Then we played arcade games. Then I won a stuffed penguin for Mary Anne

in ring toss — and she won a pair of (cheap) sunglasses for me.

We ate some homemade fudge, then some homemade taffy, then took a ride on the Ferris wheel (which was *almost* not a good idea after eating so much).

I felt like a kid again. Sea City was even more fantastic than I had expected. Mary Anne and I didn't stop laughing. I felt so close to her.

And that was when I started thinking about guess who. I know it was ridiculous, but I couldn't help it. Okay. If I were a guy, a *friend* of Mary Anne's, and we decided, hey, let's go on a *friend*ly walk, maybe ride the Ferris wheel, have a cone, visit the arcade, watch the sunset on the water. . . . Do you get the idea? I mean, you'd have to be made of cardboard not to feel all warm and lovey-dovey inside.

Wouldn't you?

I tried to put it out of my mind. I dragged Mary Anne to the Haunted House. (That took some bargaining. I had to promise to watch the glassblower afterward.) On the way there, we heard some tourists saying, "Do they dismantle the rides during a hurricane?"

That made me laugh. "Isn't it amazing?" I said. "This tropical storm is a thousand miles away, making up its mind where to go — "

"I know," Mary Anne said. "And people

135

are so sure it's going to march right into Sea City."

We stood in line and prepared for something *really* spooky. To be honest, I don't care much for haunted house-type rides. But the Tunnel of Luv was closed for repairs, so this was the next best thing.

Mary Anne looked scared. That made me smile. At least I could be reasonably sure she hadn't gone in there with — well, anyone else.

CHAPTER 14

Mallory ☺

Saturday

Dear Mrs. McGillicuddy,
    Just kidding about the name! Remember, from "I <u>Love</u> Lucy"? Anyway, your daughter is a fabulous mother's helper. The Barrett kids really love Stacey! Today was the best of all. Everyone arrived from Stoneybrook. We're taking over! They're thinking of changing the town's name to BSC City! Just kidding again. 'Bye!

                Love, Mallory

P.S. Mom and Dad send their love.

Mallory
😟

There were some things I couldn't tell Mrs. McGill in my postcard. Like how rude her daughter was being. And how wonderful that day really was.

It started out pretty typically. Beach, lunch, more beach. But Margo and Nicky got bored, so I took them into Sea City for a couple of hours.

Every few yards along the boardwalk are these binoculars, perched on swiveling posts. For a quarter, you can gaze around for about two minutes.

Nicky and Margo both wanted turns. I let them use two neighboring binoculars. "I see a kid changing *outside!*" Nicky yelled.

"Oh, yeah?" Margo replied. "Well, I see a shark."

"You do? Where?"

"You can only see it on this one."

"Oh, go wash your head in bubble gum." Nicky swung his binoculars around to look at Margo. "Ew! Ew! I see a slimy, snaggle-faced blubberfish!"

Margo pulled her face away from the binoculars and looked at Nicky. "Where? . . . Oh, you little — *Mallory!* He called me a — something bad."

I decided to change the subject. "Hey, who wants to go into town to play miniature golf?"

"Me!" they both shouted.

I don't know why I said that. The moment the words left my mouth, I regretted them. The last time the Pikes played miniature golf, we made half of Sea City mad at us for taking so many strokes to get through the course.

Oh, well, with only three of us it might not be so bad.

We left the boardwalk. When we reached the main drag, Nicky called out, "Look! Gurber Garden! Can we go in?"

"But we already ate," I replied.

"Just to *look*," Margo said, as if going to look at the inside of a hamburger place were something *everybody* did. The "Gurber Garden" was actually Claire's name for a restaurant called "Burger Garden."

"Yup, they still have that secret delicious orange sauce," Nicky the gourmet remarked when we were inside. "Mustard mixed with ketchup. They do the work *for* you."

When we came out, we saw a clown juggling on the boardwalk. He was wearing a sandwich board that said DIXIE BROTHERS CIRCUS. "Come to the circus this Sunday!" he shouted. "One day only!"

"Ooooh, can we go? Please!" the kids asked.

"We have to ask Mom and Dad," I told them. "Now, come on!"

Next stop was Fred's Putt-Putt Course. I half

expected our faces to be plastered to the walls of the rental place, like WANTED posters, reading: DO NOT RENT TO THESE PEOPLE.

But all I saw was a Sea City Savings Bank calendar and a rate schedule. I rented three putt-putt clubs, and we were off.

There was a line, not too long, made up mostly of kids. (Thank goodness. Maybe we wouldn't be the slowest ones.)

As we drew closer to the rental desk, a couple of the little boys in line began to look familiar. They turned around at the sound of a voice behind us saying, "No Coke, just 7Up and Dr Pepper!"

I spun around. Standing at a soda machine, almost hidden by the rental building, was Toby.

"Dr Pepper!" one of the boys called out.

"Me too!" the other one said.

"Can we get Dr Peppers, too? Pleeeeeease?" Margo asked.

"Sure!" I said.

What a great idea. I was happy to go to the machine.

As I walked to it, I said, "Hi." (Not original, I know.)

"Oh, hi, uh — wait, don't tell me . . . *Mallory*!" Toby said.

He remembered! "Right . . . Toby," I replied.

"Hey, we're batting a thousand! Can I get your sodas? I have lots of quarters."

"No, that's okay," I said.

I noticed Toby had two Dr Peppers and one 7Up. I made sure to get the same.

While I was putting the money in, he *waited* for me. He waited to walk me back to the line!

I mean, it was only about twenty steps, but still I could tell Toby was a sweet guy.

Toby's charges, Ben and Peter, were eight and six years old. They'd already met Nicky and Margo at the beach. The four kids were blabbering away like old friends.

"Hey, we're next for rentals," Toby said.

"Uh-huh," I replied.

"Why don't we do this together?"

"Okay."

I was dying for him to ask me something that wasn't a yes-or-no question. I was sure he thought I was a total no-brain.

But I had nothing to worry about. We spent a long, long afternoon together. Well, not really *together*, because Toby spent a lot of time helping Ben and Peter with their technique. (Boys can be very competitive, even at miniature golf.) Nicky and Margo kept looking at them, trying to imitate everything Toby was doing.

Me? I'm a pretty good golfer, if I do say so

myself. I just played quietly, and helped the kids if they asked.

Toby would smile at me once in awhile and wink. It always, always made me blush. Which I *hate*. I have red hair and freckles to begin with, so I look like a ripe, hairy tomato when I blush.

When we were at the "Old King Cole Hole," Toby said, "Have you taken lessons or something?"

"No," I answered, ripening again. "I just aim and hit."

He crouched next to me, imitating my stance. "Now, let's see, your shoulders are like this, right?"

We talked a lot. The kids played well — but cheated a lot, which was all right because it made the game go faster.

At the end, we all walked home together. Ben and Peter insisted on playing leap frog with Margo and Nicky.

Toby and I couldn't help laughing. "Kids are a handful," Toby said.

I rolled my eyes. "Try living with seven of them — brothers and sisters, I mean."

Toby let out a low whistle. "It must be crazy. Do your parents give you a break — like, time off from helpering?"

I shrugged. "They do, if I ask."

"Oh. Well, would you like to *ask* about Friday evening?"

For a moment the words just hung in the air. I felt as if I were walking around them. Looking at them. Making sure they were the ones I had heard. Making sure I knew their meaning.

Then my stomach did a flip-flop. Toby was asking me out! Wasn't he?

"Um, Friday evening?" My voice sounded as if I'd just swallowed some helium.

"Yeah. I have the evening off. And I wasn't planning anything, so I thought maybe you and I could . . . you know, go out. If you want."

Yes! *Yes! YES!* He *was* asking!

My mouth answered before my brain could think another thought. "Well, sure, Toby. I'd love to!"

"Great! I'll pick you up at seven at your place?"

"Okay!"

He looked at his watch. "Ugh, I'm late. I have to rush. See you Friday!" He ran off and pulled his charges away from their game.

As they disappeared down the beach, I thought I would just float away with happiness.

"Come on," I managed to say to Margo and

Nicky. "Let's change for dinner."

They raced each other to the house. I pinched myself. It wasn't a dream. It had happened.

It felt as if a hummingbird were fluttering around in my heart. I wanted to scream, but too many people were around. So I squeaked. I didn't care who heard me.

I had to tell Jessi.

I flew to the house. I could hear the kids inside changing. I bounded upstairs, ran straight into the room, and slammed the door.

"Mallory!" Jessi gasped. "You scared me."

I plopped on my bed and said, "Oh, Jessi Jessi Jessi Jessi Jessi Jessi!"

"What what what what what? Are you okay?"

"No." I shook my head and looked her straight in the eye. "I'm in love."

CHAPTER 15

Dawn

Sunday

Dear Mom and Richard,
　　Where is the summer? Today we had to wear jackets! Boy, were we lucky. We found something to do indoors. A circus! And I don't mean the Pikes' house.
　　This one only had one ring, and it was much quieter.

See you in a week,
Dawn

Dawn

"Arrrrrgggghhh!"

There was a creature in the bathroom. It was communicating in no language known to humankind. But one thing was clear. It brought a message of great annoyance.

Suddenly it appeared at my bedroom door. It held up a piece of wet rectangular pink fabric. "The pink one is mine!" it said. "The green one is yours."

It then stormed away to the bathroom.

"I know," I replied.

"Good. Then would you mind wiping your face on *your* towel next time?"

I went to the bathroom. "Stacey, I *did* wipe my face on my towel. Maybe one of the kids used your towel. Don't forget, there are six new people in the house this weekend."

"No kidding. And everyone has decided to wipe their hands and faces on *my* towel."

Oh, boy. Talk about waking up on the wrong side of the bed.

I sighed. Maybe it was the weather. Sunday was cool and gray. Definitely not a beach day.

Moments earlier, Mrs. Barrett had stopped by our room. She said she and Franklin wanted to take the kids on a trip to Smithtown, a restored Colonial village nearby, if it didn't rain.

The way Stacey was acting, I was glad we'd be away from the house, in a public place.

Then *maybe* she'd be on her best behavior.

What had caused the sea change in Stacey? (Don't you love that expression, "sea change"? Mary Anne's dad uses it to mean a humongous change. I figured it was appropriate here in Sea City.) I knew things weren't going great for Stacey. She'd been a little distant the day before. She'd complained about Mrs. Barrett. She had said she missed being a mother's helper at the Pikes'. And she was *not* pleased when Mallory came home all starry-eyed about Toby. Neither of us could believe he'd asked her out on a date.

Still, I couldn't see how any of these things, especially that last thing, would bother Stacey. She couldn't stand Toby. She'd said so. Often.

"Stace?" I asked, standing in the bathroom door. "Are you mad about something besides the towel?"

"No. What should I be mad about?"

She began brushing her teeth furiously.

"Well, I thought maybe you were thinking about . . . you know, Toby and Mallory."

Stacey laughed. The mirror became polka-dotted with flecks of toothpaste. "Are you kidding? She can have him!"

"That's what I thought."

Brush, brush, brush, spit. "He's just going to treat her like a disposable dishrag."

"Yeah."

147

Rinse, rinse, rinse, spit. "I told her, but she wouldn't listen to me."

"I remember."

Gargle, gargle, gargle, spit. "Anyway, I couldn't care less what they do. Now let's go downstairs, before Mrs. Barrett has one of her fits."

"Okay."

We dressed quickly and ran downstairs. The kids were already up, which made me feel a little guilty.

"But I don't *want* to go to yucky, boring Smithtown!" Buddy's voice rang out from the kitchen.

Everyone was crowded around the table. Franklin was at the stove making omelets. And Mrs. Barrett was looking annoyed. "How do you know it's boring?" she asked.

"It just *is!*" Suzi chimed in. "Today's Sunday, and that's the day of the Dixie Circus!"

"Yeah, we want to go there!" Lindsey said.

When Franklin saw us, he shouted, "Hey, girls, what do you want in your omelets? We have cheese, mushrooms, pepperoni, anchovies, prunes, raisins, chicken nuggets, chocolate chips — "

He began dancing around, throwing ingredients in the omelet pan.

"Franklin, stop!" Mrs. Barrett said, laughing.

Stacey didn't crack a smile.

Despite Franklin's comedy act, the Smithtown versus Dixie Brothers debate continued. Finally, in the middle of breakfast, Mrs. Barrett said, "Enough! Franklin, why don't you and I drop the kids off at the circus with Dawn and Stacey. We'll go on to Smithtown and pick them up afterward. Okay?"

"Yeeeaaaaa!"

A very wise decision had been made. I was actually glad to be going to the circus. I just hoped the Dixie Brothers could pull Stacey out of her bad mood.

Well, I guess when I had heard the name "Dixie Brothers," I had thought of "Ringling Brothers." I wasn't expecting just a little tent in a vacant lot at the edge of town. Outside the tent were a few rides and concession stands. It was very . . . *temporary-*looking.

As we waited in line to buy tickets, we saw a life-sized statue of a pirate propped up against a tent post. He had a wicked smile and a patch over one eye, and a hairy wart at the end of his nose.

"That is so lifelike," Lindsey said, walking over to it.

"Is it part of the circus?" Buddy asked.

"Sure is!" a clown shouted from behind us.

"We just bought it from Madame Trousseau's Wax Museum!"

"Really?" Taylor said. He stepped up close to it, followed by the rest of the kids.

Stacey and I stayed in line. "Don't break it," Stacey warned them.

Buddy touched its costume, then reached toward its face. "I just want to touch its wart!" he said.

Suddenly the statue slapped Buddy's hand away. "Arrrghhh! Blimey, a mate can't get a rest on dry land around these parts," he snarled.

"AAAAAAGGGHHH!" Buddy, Suzi, Lindsey, Taylor, and Madeleine all screamed and backed away. Ryan and Marnie burst into tears and ran into our arms.

Then, with a smile and a wave, the pirate said, "Top of the mornin' to ya, mates," and walked away.

The clown bounded up to us and patted the two little ones on the head. Then he grinned and said, "Expect the unexpected at the Dixie Brothers!"

As he walked away, his pants fell down. Instantly Marnie and Ryan began to giggle.

"He was real all the time!" Lindsey said.

"Yeah, he was tricking us!" Buddy realized.

"A pretty cheap trick, I thought," Stacey said.

Dawn

We bought our tickets and saw the show. How was it? Well, honestly, not great. There was one ring, and a few tired animals performing tricks. The trapeze act was scary, but mostly because it looked like the flimsy tent was going to fall down. And the sword swallower actually swallowed a flame-tipped saber (I have never figured out how they do that). The clowns were okay, and the pirate walked around and tried to be scary while the clowns kicked him.

From the kids' reaction, you'd have thought we were at the Big Top. They *adored* the show! When it was over, they ran outside and begged us to take them on rides.

As Stacey and I kept an eye on them, I bought us some pretzels. She took one bite of hers and said, "You know what I really want? Some peanuts — the kind that are in their shells."

I didn't really feel like going back to the end of the line at the food stand. But I wanted to make Stacey happy. "You stay here and watch the kids," I said. "I'll get some."

"Thanks, Dawn."

Well, guess what? I couldn't find any peanuts except the sugared, shelled kind. "No luck," I said to Stacey. "I guess they don't have them here."

Stacey looked at me blankly. "Yes they do. I saw some."

Then *she* went looking. When she came back, her brow was all creased. "I could have sworn I saw people eating some. Oh, this is so depressing. I have *such* a craving."

Stacey began to sulk. I tried to make conversation with her, but it wasn't easy. She seemed awfully upset about the peanuts.

When Franklin and Mrs. Barrett came back, I felt relieved. On the way home, the kids chattered on and on about the circus. I added a thing or two, but Stacey just stared out the window.

"We heard some exciting news in Smithtown," Franklin said at one point. "Some of the stores in Sea City are stocking up on supplies — bottled water, batteries, canned goods — in case the hurricane hits."

"Why?" Lindsey asked.

"Well, the old-timers remember how the causeway washed out in the last hurricane," Franklin replied.

"Oh, no!" Suzi said.

"Don't worry, sweetheart," Mrs. Barrett said with a chuckle. "That was years ago, before they could build strong roads, and before they had big speedboats that could take supplies back and forth."

"Besides," Franklin said, "there's no hurricane anyway, just some storm down near Jamaica. And the weatherman says it's going to be hot and sunny tomorrow, with no clouds."

"A beach day?" Buddy asked.

"Well, yeah," Franklin replied. "For all you lucky Barrett kids."

"Yippeee!"

Me? I was looking forward to the next day, too. I felt as if I'd been baby-sitting for eight kids that day. Tomorrow the Harrises would leave, and I would move to the Pikes'.

Then I could have a *real* vacation.

16

Mary Anne

Tuesday

Dear Logan,
Are you feeling better today than you were yesterday? I hope so. You looked so sad.

Not that I was a perfect specimen. I hope I didn't cry too much. I miss you SOOO much!

I saw Alex and Toby today. They really liked you. (They thought you looked like Cam Geary, too, so there!)

Oh, guess what? I may be coming home sooner than expected. We may be getting that storm after all.

Love always,
Mary Anne

Mary Anne

Poor Logan. Sunday he had told me a little about his job at the Rosebud Cafe. He's their youngest busboy, but he's so good that they give him twice as much work to do. Added to that, lunch business is booming. (Probably because of all the girls who show up just to look at him.)

But we had the best visit. Sea City has become a special place for me, and it was wonderful sharing it with him. I think he had a good time, too. He loved the boardwalk and the beach.

It was funny, though. Sometimes he just wasn't *himself*. He'd draw inward, which isn't like Logan at all. I thought it might have had something to do with Alex. Logan seemed a little uncomfortable meeting him.

I asked Logan about his moods. He assured me he was just thinking about having to go back to Stoneybrook on Monday.

Sigh. I sure did know how he felt. I wished his visit could have lasted a week. I felt *miserable* when he left. As usual, I started blubbering. And as usual, my friends teased me about it. Dawn handed me a Kleenex, but it got sopping wet. So Kristy handed me a beach towel.

He left about noon with the Harrises. The day was bright and sunny, and we spent the rest of it on the beach. The Big Event was a fight between Buddy and Nicky. They were building a castle together and Nicky was in charge of putting water in the moat.

SPLASH! He dumped in a pailful and went back for more.

"Hey!" Buddy shouted, "You busted the drawbridge!"

Nicky turned around and stared blankly.

"I spent *hours* on that," Buddy went on. "You fix it."

"I didn't mean to break it," Nicky said. *"You* fix it!"

"You broke it."

"You should have made it stronger!"

"Fix it, Nicky-Nicky-Got-So-Sicky!"

"No, Buddy-Buddy-Elmer-Fuddy!"

Nicky picked up a fistful of sand and threw it in Buddy's face. With an ear-splitting scream, Buddy covered his eyes. "Owww! He got *sand* in my eyes!"

Stacey rushed to Buddy. Mallory rushed to Nicky.

"He started it," Nicky said.

"Ow! Ow! Ow! Ow! It hurts!" Buddy screamed.

Stacey calmly walked him into knee-deep water and tried to rinse his eyes. "It's okay. You'll be all right . . ."

Mal gave Nicky a scolding. Then she took him by the hand and walked toward Stacey. "Is he okay?" she called out.

"Fine," Stacey snapped. "Mal, can't you or Jessi keep a closer eye on these kids? They shouldn't throw sand!"

"I'm sorry," Mal said.

"What planet were you on, anyway? Or were you too busy with . . . with fantasies of older boys?"

Whoa. That did not sound like Stacey. Poor Mallory didn't know what had hit her. I could see her eyes water, so I took her for a long walk.

Later Stacey apologized (thank goodness). Honestly, I didn't know what had gotten into her.

The next day, Tuesday, started out nice but became cloudy and cool around noon. Buddy, Suzi, Vanessa, Margo, Marnie, and Claire insisted on building sand castles, even in the overcast weather. The triplets and Nicky wanted to go into town and see a double feature of *Robin Hood* and *The Sword in the Stone*.

Mal and Jessi agreed to stay at the beach, and Stacey went to the movies. She and Mal, needless to say, were barely talking.

As for us "guests"? Kristy and Dawn stayed

with the beach crowd, and the rest of us went to the theater.

Afterward, as we were gabbing about Prince John's death scene, Claudia said, "Is it Sunday or something?"

"Huh?" I asked.

Claudia pointed to the road. "Look at all these cars."

The street was bumper to bumper. "That's weird," Stacey said. "Maybe a lot of people had four-day weekends."

We didn't give it much more thought, until we returned to the Pikes'. There, Mr. and Mrs. Pike were sitting in the kitchen with Mrs. Barrett. They looked very serious.

"They say the road was fortified a few years ago," Mrs. Barrett was saying.

"They said the *Titanic* was unsinkable," Mr. Pike replied.

"Is the *Titanic* going through the marsh?" Claudia asked.

We all cracked up. "No," Mrs. Pike said. "We're just talking strategy in case Hurricane Bill hits."

"There *is* going to be a hurricane?" Stacey asked.

Mr. Pike shrugged. "Nobody can tell. The storm is gathering force off the coast of Florida, and it's expected to blow north. It could blow out to sea, or just fizzle."

"Or it could hit the Jersey coast, right?" Stacey said.

"It could," Mrs. Barrett answered. "But if that happened, it wouldn't be until tomorrow night or Thursday morning, at the earliest."

"Stores are stocking up in case we're cut off from the mainland," Mrs. Pike added.

"Some people down the road are boarding up their windows," Mr. Pike said.

"This'll be great!" Adam blurted out. "We can stay inside, tell stories and eat Spam and tuna fish and fruit cocktail."

"I'm scared," Byron said, standing close to his mom.

"Is a hurricane like a tornado?" Nicky asked.

"No, sweetheart," Mrs. Pike said. "It's a very, very windy rainstorm."

"Well, if it is going to come, we should think seriously of going home beforehand," Mrs. Barrett suggested.

"The weather people have only called a hurricane *watch*," Mr. Pike answered. "That means there's a possibility it'll come. Maybe fifty-fifty, maybe less. A hurricane *warning* means there's a good chance."

Mrs. Pike exhaled. "I don't know. It *is* only a *watch*, and we have the house till Saturday. It would be a shame to give it up for nothing."

No one said a thing for a few minutes. Me?

I was hoping we'd stay. I agreed with Mrs. Pike.

Finally Mrs. Barrett said, "I think you're right. It's not worth giving up our vacation for a fifty-fifty chance. We just have to be prepared."

Mr. Pike stood up from the table. "Then it's settled. I'll go into town and get supplies, just in case." He grabbed a pad and pen from near the phone. "Now, what do I need to get? Bottled water, canned goods — "

"Flashlights and batteries," Mrs. Pike said. "Candles, maybe a battery-operated radio and clock — "

"Candy and cookies!" Jordan suggested.

"Can I go with you?" Adam asked.

"Me too!" the other boys screamed.

I was starting to feel tingly inside.

This was getting exciting.

CHAPTER 17

Jessi

Wednesday

Dear Mama and
Daddy,
Wish me luck. It
is eight o-clock in
the morning, and
Claire and Margo
have been up for
hours. They are
determined to win
the Sea City Sand
Castle Contest. That
is a little like
Daddy entering the
New York City Ballet
competition planning
to win it (no
offense, Daddy). The
other contestants are

pros! I think they plan to live in their castles year-round.

Oh, well. I can handle a few tearful kids ... can't I? After all, I am a Super Sitter.

Love and kisses,
Jessi

This Sitter was not feeling very Super on Wednesday. Especially at six in the morning.

That was when I felt the earthquake. Well, in my dream it was an earthquake. I was dancing on stage with the American Ballet Theater. Suddenly I felt my body bounce around. Then the floor opened up. I looked down and saw the orchestra falling into a big hole. One of the violinists was shouting, "Can we go make castles now?"

That's when I opened my eyes and saw Claire Pike. She was jumping up and down on my bed. Margo was doing the same, on Mallory's bed.

"Can we?" Claire repeated.

Jessi

"You sound just like the violinist," I said with a yawn.

"Huh?"

"Never mind." I looked out the window. It was *dark*. It was also cloudy and cold and gloomy. The kind of morning that makes any normal person want to sleep late.

I plopped back in bed and said, "It's way too early, you guys. The contest doesn't begin for four hours. Can't you wait awhile?"

"Ohhhhhhh," Margo started to moan.

"Come on," I heard Mallory say. "You can practice in front of the house, okay? Just let us sleep."

"But we've been practicing for days!" Margo complained.

"Well . . . go have breakfast," Mal said. "Do *something*. Just let us sleep."

That worked for awhile. Sort of. *Mal* slept. I tried, but I kept thinking of that earthquake. Then I'd hear bumps and giggles downstairs and feel as if I wasn't doing my job.

Finally I went downstairs and helped the kids fix their breakfast. Then, while they played outside, I wrote a postcard in the living room.

Before long, the rest of the family was up. I, Super Sitter, went to work. I made pancakes, poured cereal, cleaned spills, and washed dishes.

"Jessi, you are amazing," Mrs. Pike said at one point.

Boy, was I glad to hear that. I almost forgot how tired I was.

When Mal came downstairs to help, things became easier — although Margo and Claire could hardly sit still. Every few minutes, Claire would run inside and ask, "What time is it now?" One of us would answer, for instance, "Eight twenty-seven," and she'd say, "How many more minutes till ten o'clock?"

By nine-thirty I'd had enough. "Okay, Claire and Margo. Let's go for it!"

"Yeeaaaaaa!" Claire screamed.

"We're going to win!" Margo yelled.

I gritted my teeth and tried to smile. I was hoping they'd want to enter the contest for *fun*. I was hoping they weren't serious about "going for the gold."

But I was wrong. And I knew I'd have a few broken hearts to mend in a couple of hours.

"Good luck!" Mal said. "I'll bring the others down a little later."

"Great!" I replied. I stepped outside to see what the weather was like.

Still dreary and chilly. "You guys," I said, "go get your windbreakers." I got mine, too, and we shoved off. Margo and Claire were loaded up with tools — plastic buckets, shovels, pails, and a bag full of seashells to use as decorations.

We walked next door to pick up Suzi (Stacey stayed with Buddy and Marnie). Suzi came running out with a shopping bag full of her equipment.

Mrs. Barrett and Stacey waved good-bye. "I'll come with my camera!" Mrs. Barrett shouted.

Fine, I thought. As long as she got pictures of them *before* the results were announced.

We walked toward the north jetty. I had to bundle myself up tightly against the cold. I looked to the horizon, but the sun wasn't peeking in anywhere.

"Aren't you cold?" I asked the girls.

"A little," Margo said.

"When you start getting wet," I said, "you're really going to feel it."

"That's okay," Claire piped up.

"You're sure you don't want to stay home, have some hot chocolate, maybe read a story — "

"*No!*" was the unanimous reply.

I gave up. There was no turning back now.

We walked to the lifeguard stand. Two very adorable, muscular guys were standing on it. "Hi," one of them said.

"Hi," I answered. "We came to sign up."

The guys looked at each other, then back at us. "Sign up? You mean, for the castle contest?"

"Yeah!" Margo said.

"Oh, that's been canceled because of the storm," the second lifeguard said. "They're going to hold it next week — Wednesday, I think."

Margo dropped her equipment in the sand. "Ohhhhhh!" she groaned.

"Lifeguard-silly-billy-goo-goo," Claire said under her breath.

"Yeah," Suzi agreed, thrusting out her lower lip.

Next week! Whoa, I was saved! We'd be miles away by then.

I looked around. The beach was *empty*. I'd barely noticed. In fact, I'd sort of forgotten about Hurricane Bill, Tropical Storm Bill, or whatever it was.

"So what about some hot chocolate?" I said.

"Yeah!" The girls started running back.

You know what I decided? Hurricane or storm, Bill was my hero.

167

CHAPTER 18

Claudia

Wednesday

Dear Carley,
   Oh, I hop this card gets to you. This hole place is in a panick. You woldnt belive it its like a movie. In fact I'm writting this in the car, stuck in traffic. Sea city is being evakiu avaydat cleared out because of the hurrycan.
   Its exiting but scary. What if we all get blowk away?
   Oh well, if I die, you can have all my art equiptment!

                    Love always,
                    Claudia
P.S. Just jocking, dont worry. (I think)

Our ears were plastered to the radio. (Wait. Ew. What an image. Oh, well. You know what I mean.)

"To repeat, the hurricane watch has become a hurricane warning. The tropical storm is now officially Hurricane Bill. Coastal-flood and small-craft warnings are in effect, for winds up to one hundred miles an hour. Residents are advised to stay away from coastal and outlying areas. All New Jersey beaches are closed. We have reports that Bill is already creating extensive damage along the North Carolina shore and should arrive in New Jersey this evening, after which he will proceed up the East Coast. . . ."

Mrs. Pike turned down the radio. All of us — kids, grown-ups, Barretts, Pikes — were crowded in the kitchen. Outside the rain was already pounding against the window.

"Well," she said, "what do we do now?"

Mr. Pike scratched his chin. "We can't stay here. A beach is the worst place to be in a hurricane."

Poor Byron's lower lip was trembling. "Are we going to die?"

Mrs. Pike smiled and hugged him tight. "Absolutely, positively not."

(Byron looked happier. I wasn't so convinced.)

"But I'm not so sure it's a great idea to pack

169

up and return home," Mr. Pike said.

"Honey," Mrs. Pike replied, "three days of vacation time is not as important as — "

"I'm not thinking of the vacation," Mr. Pike said. "I wonder how smart it is to try to drive to Connecticut. We'll be in the hurricane's path the whole way, in heavy traffic, with no visibility — most of the trip will be at night."

Then Kristy spoke up. "We'd be better off just moving inland, to a motel or something."

Leave it to Kristy. *One* statement, and we have a perfect solution to the Problem of the Year.

"That's a good idea," Mr. Pike said. He glanced out the window, then looked sternly around the room. "Now listen. I want everybody to pack just a few clothes into overnight bags. Enough for two days, tops. *And I don't want any fighting.* This is very serious. We'll meet back here in fifteen minutes. Now, go."

We went. Fast. I have hardly ever heard quiet, easy-going Mr. Pike talk like that.

Kristy and I ran to the room we shared. Kristy threw a pair of underwear, some socks, and a T-shirt into a backpack. "Come on," she said.

I was having a dilemma. I was wearing the only long pants I had packed, these overdyed navy jeans. I was also wearing a loose black cotton sweater over a white tank top. So if I packed my big purple Hawaiian shorts, which were the next warmest pants, I'd be stuck having to wear an *orange* striped shirt, which was the only long-sleeved one I'd brought. Unless I wore the sweater again over it. . . .

"Uh, Claud?" Kristy said. "Bill is a hurricane, you know — not a fashion-show judge."

"I know, I know. You go ahead. I'll be right down."

Clomp-clomp-clomp-clomp. Kristy was the first one downstairs. "Someone should call Stoneybrook!" I heard her yell.

I ended up packing three outfits — one in case it was cold and rainy, one in case it was warm and rainy, and one really nice one to change into if necessary (or if the weather cleared up). I thought that was very sensible.

Oh, and some extra shoes and a big bag of Mars bars I'd stashed away for a rainy day.

When I got downstairs, everyone's luggage was piled in the kitchen — along with beach equipment and chairs.

Dawn ran inside, soaked. She was carrying two folded-up beach umbrellas. "We're bringing everything inside, so it won't blow around."

In the living room Mr. and Mrs. Pike were setting down the wicker swing from the porch. "I think this is it," Mrs. Pike called out.

"Is there anything else we need to do?" I heard Kristy ask.

"Well, I called Ellen Cooke at the real estate office, and she said to close the faucets and shut the circuit breakers," Mrs. Pike said. "And board or tape up the windows."

I had a sinking feeling. There are, like, a hundred and fifty windows in that house. And the weather was getting worse by the minute.

"I don't think we can worry about the windows now," Mr. Pike said. "It looks like the whole neighborhood is clearing out, and we're going to hit major traffic. I'll deal with the circuit breakers. You all get into the cars now."

Aye, aye, Captain Pike! (No, don't worry, I just *thought* that. I didn't say it.)

I took my suitcase and ran outside. It was *pouring*. I could barely open my eyes.

"In here!" Kristy called from the van. I followed her voice and jumped in.

"You sure you packed enough?" she asked as she hauled my suitcase into the back storage area.

I shook myself off and looked around. Mallory and Jessi were in the front seat. Mary Anne, Dawn, Margo, and Claire were squeezed in the middle seat. That left the long backseat for Nicky, Vanessa, Kristy, and me.

I could see Mr. Pike running toward the Barretts' station wagon. He shouted, "How many do you have?"

Mrs. Pike's voice shouted back, "Nine!" (The Barretts and the rest of the Pikes were traveling together.)

Mr. Pike climbed into the driver's seat and counted us. "Eleven!" he shouted out the window. "Let's move it!"

Vrrrooom! The engine started. I looked at Kristy. This tiny smile was on her face. I could tell she wanted to do just what I wanted to do.

Squeal.

This was very, very exciting.

"Where are we going, Daddy?" Margo asked as we pulled out of the driveway.

"I don't know, honey," he said. "The first place on the mainland where we can find vacancies."

Mr. Pike drove sloooowly down the street. He put the windshield wipers on the fastest speed, but they didn't help. The rain drenched the window right after each wipe.

"Can't see a blessed thing," he muttered.

Somehow he found his way into downtown Sea City. It looked like a ghost town — a soggy ghost town. Most of the shop windows were covered by big wooden boards. Either that or huge *X*'s made of thick tape.

The traffic was very heavy. Horns blared left and right. We slowed to a stop as we approached the causeway.

Soon we could see flashing red lights everywhere.

"What's going on?" Kristy asked.

Mr. Pike rolled down the window and stuck out his head. "Here comes a policeman," he said.

We leaned forward to listen. I could feel my heart pounding. Were they letting cars over the causeway one at a time? Had a car spun out and crashed?

"Excuse me!" Mr. Pike shouted. "Can you tell me what happened?"

A policeman in a rain suit and boots appeared by the window. "Causeway's underwater!" He had to yell to be heard over the rain.

"You mean *no one* can leave the island?" Mr. Pike asked.

"That's right, sir! I'm awaiting further instructions."

He vanished. Mr. Pike rolled up the window and sank into his seat.

Vanessa started to cry. "Daddy, are we going to be in a flood?"

"No, sweetheart, they're going to tell us where to go."

"But we're stranded!" Margo said. "The hurricane's going to get us!"

She burst into tears, which made Nicky sob, too.

Oh, my lord. This was not fun at all. My mouth was feeling dry. I wanted to open the door and run. I felt trapped. Another few minutes of this rain and the van was going to turn into an ark. If it didn't sink.

I was about to scream when the policeman ran to the van again. Ahead of us I could see cars moving to the side of the road, making U-turns.

"Sir!" he yelled. "We've been instructed to tell everyone remaining here to take shelter in the elementary school. Turn around here and go three blocks to Cottage Road, then turn right. The school's on top of the hill."

"Thanks!" Mr. Pike backed the van up and turned around. His eyes were glued to the rearview mirror. "Come on," he mumbled. "Stick with us."

Slowly we inched our way across town. The rain pounded like war drums on the roof.

Or maybe that was the sound of my own heart.

CHAPTER 19

Stacey

Dear Mom,

I am writing this by flashlight. We are all in the gym of the Sea City Elementary School. I know you must be worried about me. You've probably been hearing about Hurricane Bill, and how the causeway got washed out. Well, we're safe and dry. This building is like a fortress.

I will mail this tomorrow. I heard they're going to send a mail <u>boat</u> to the mainland after the hurricane passes

I love you. Don't worry.

Your stranded daughter,

Stacey

"I can't see the street signs!" Mrs. Barrett said, squinting through the front window.

"Just follow the van's tail lights," Mrs. Pike said calmly.

"Are . . . are . . . are . . ."

Poor, frightened Suzi was curled up in my lap. Her question was coming out in gasping sobs.

"Are we lost?" she finally asked.

"No, we're almost there," I said reassuringly.

Did I believe that? No way. I was scared out of my mind. I thought we'd never reach the school. I was sure the water would rise up and carry us into the ocean.

To our left, Adam stared glumly out the window. "This stinks," he grumbled. In the back section of the station wagon, Byron and Jordan agreed with him.

Buddy and Marnie were in the front seat, bawling their eyes out. Mrs. Pike held Marnie in her lap and gently stroked her hair. Somehow she managed to put her left arm around Buddy's shoulders. "Rain, rain, go away," she began to sing, "come again some other day."

I was very happy Mrs. Pike was in the car. I don't know what I'd have done if Mrs. Barrett were the only grown-up there. I think she was the only person more scared of the hurricane than I was.

Mrs. Barrett steered the car to the right. We began climbing the hill to the school. Next to us, a couple of people were *pushing* a car up the hill. "Ugh, what a time to have engine trouble," Mrs. Pike said.

She was trying to sound light-hearted, to make everything seem more normal.

But there was nothing normal about a hurricane. And there was certainly nothing normal about being stranded on an island at sea.

It seemed like hours before we finally approached a parking lot. It was jammed. "Where on earth are we supposed to park this thing?" Mrs. Barrett said.

"I think anywhere's fine. Just pull over to the side of the road. Let's get inside," replied Mrs. Pike.

Mrs. Barrett did so. We hopped out of the car.

It was like being under attack. It felt as if all the water in the world had been collected in one huge bucket and dumped over Sea City. I was drenched in about two seconds as I ran to the back of the car.

I yanked the door open. "You guys take your stuff and stick close to your mom!" I shouted to the triplets.

As Byron and Jordan scrambled out, I grabbed as many bags as I could. The two moms were herding the rest of the kids out of the car.

"I'm going to take Marnie inside!" Mrs. Barrett yelled, scooping her into her arms. "Stacey, you follow me with Buddy and Suzi!"

"Okay!" I replied. I grabbed Suzi's hand. Buddy was right by my side with his backpack.

"We'll get the rest of the bags!" Mrs. Pike shouted.

Nobody was crying now. We needed all our energy just to put one foot in front of the other. The wind was like a big hand trying to push us back down the hill.

Somehow we reached the side door of the school. We stepped inside onto a filthy, wet linoleum floor. The noise was deafening, between the rain drumming against the windows and the people shouting.

I pulled my hair back and squeezed out as much water as I could. My charges were all with me, safe and sound. That was my first concern. They'd started crying again — but so had about a hundred other kids around us.

Mrs. Barrett was hugging Marnie. I crouched down and put my arms around Buddy and Suzi. "We're safe now," I repeated over and over.

I looked around. We were in a gymnasium. The windows had been boarded up from the outside. Some of the boards were rattling in the wind. At the far end of the gym, people were setting up cots with blankets. A small group valiantly tried to mop water off the floor. In the midst of it all, a man in raingear was shouting something into a bullhorn.

Pandemonium. Total, utter chaos. No wonder the kids were screaming.

"Remind you of the SES sleepover?"

I looked up to see Dawn smiling at me. Just beyond her were the other members of the BSC and the rest of the Pike family. I felt awfully relieved.

"Yeah," I said, "except ours was noisier!"

Dawn laughed.

"Quiet, please! May I have everybody's attention?" The man with the bullhorn was finally managing to be heard over the din. "With the help of the local Red Cross, we are in the process of setting up sleeping cots. If any of you have dry sleeping bags, it would help us greatly if you'd use them. Now, we have a team of volunteers preparing food in the cafeteria, which is down the hall. I can't promise a gourmet meal, but there's ample canned food for everyone here. And as long as the refrigeration holds out, I believe we have some ice cream for the children!"

Boy, did he know the right thing to say. All those crying kids were suddenly buzzing with excitement.

"So settle in, have some grub, and make some new friends," he continued. "We may be spending quite a bit of time together."

I heard a smattering of applause. The sound level rose again, but not nearly as high. A lot more people were smiling, and many were shaking hands and chatting.

Mr. Pike waved us all toward him. "Okay, let's have a strategy meeting."

"I want ice cream!" Claire said.

"I know you do," Mr. Pike replied. "We'll go to the cafeteria as soon as we stake out some cots. I see quite a few empties in the far corner, so let's go over there!"

We picked up our bags and ran. In no time we had staked out a sleeping corner of our own. All the kids (and most of us BSCers) got cots. The grown-ups, Kristy, and Mal agreed to sleep on the floor on blankets.

As for dinner, well, it was divine. I had a savory helping of canned deviled ham, garnished with canned lima beans (in their own juice). My beverage? A V8 juice cocktail. Topping it off was a stick of sugar-free peppermint gum courtesy of our private confectioner, Claudia Kishi.

I have to admit, there *was* something exciting in the air. The kids were screaming and scarfing down food like crazy.

When it was time to head back to the gym,

181

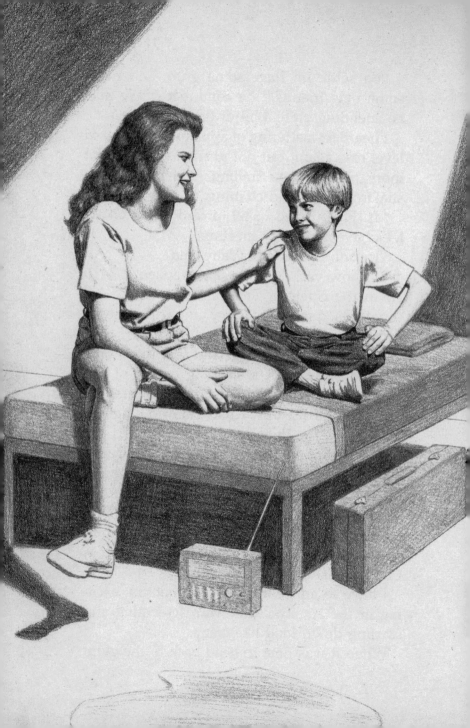

Stacey

I took Suzi and Marnie's hands. Suzi seemed agitated. "What's up?" I asked.

"I didn't bring my pj's," she mumbled.

"Me neither," Buddy said.

"Me threether," Adam chimed in.

"That's okay," I cut in before we got any fourther. (Sorry.) "I think we can sleep in our clothes tonight."

"Yippeeeee!" cried the kids. (Isn't it amazing what kids find exciting and fun? Just thinking about sleeping in my clothes made me feel grungy.)

When we were halfway across the gym, the lights went out.

Just like that. No warning, no sound, no electrical *dzzzzit*, nothing.

Everyone in the gym fell silent for a moment. Then I heard some baffled mumbling, then some groans, and people calling out for lost family members.

"Mom?" said Nicky's timid voice.

"Stick together, everyone," Mr. Pike said firmly. "Hold hands and follow my voice."

Suddenly about six sets of emergency lights popped on. They cast pools of dull amber light around the gym.

Slowly we made our way to the cots.

"Uh, it looks like we lost some power, folks," the man said through the bullhorn. "We'll be passing out candles and flashlights in a moment, so just sit tight."

Fortunately the Pikes had remembered to bring flashlights of their own — and a radio. Mr. Pike shone his light from cot to cot and blanket to blanket. "Everybody here? Ready for sleep?"

I heard nineteen yeses. Everyone was being so obedient and quiet. I stretched out, exhausted. What a day!

And then . . .

"Mommy, Buddy kicked me!"

"Hey, that's *my* backpack!"

"Shhh, I want to sleep!"

The members of the BSC went to work. "Kids, come on now . . ."

Oh, well. It was nice to know, in the middle of one of the worst storms of all time, that some things hadn't changed.

CHAPTER 20

KAREN

THURSDAY

DEAR GRANNY AND GRANDAD,
   WERE YOU EVER IN A HURRICANE? I WAS! ITS NAME
WAS HURRICANE BILL. IT CAME THROUGH STONEY BROOK
THIS MORNING (WHEN IT WAS STILL DARK). BUT I WAS
AWAKE! BOY, WAS IT SCARY! BUT WE'RE ALL ALIVE. OUR
HOUSE DIDN'T BLOW AWAY. NOW IT'S SUNNY. I HOPE WE
GET ANOTHER HURRICANE SOMEDAY. MAYBE YOU COULD
COME VISIT AND SEE IT.

LOVE, KAREN

You know what? I had a secret wish. My secret wish was that Hurricane Bill would pick up our house and take it to Nebraska. That is where Granny and Grandad live.

It would be like the opposite of *The Wizard of Oz.* We would start off in a colorful place, Stoneybrook. And we would end up on a farm.

And we would not have to pay for plane tickets.

Well, it did not really happen that way.

The excitement started Wednesday. That was when my stepsister, Kristy, called her mother to tell her about the hurricane.

Kristy's mother, Elizabeth, is married to my Daddy. They live in this gigundo house. My brother Andrew and I live there, too, every other weekend. The rest of the time we live with Mommy and my stepfather, Seth. Our house (Mommy and Seth's) is little. But it is also in Stoneybrook.

Anyway, we were in the little house when Kristy called the big house. The reason I know was because Elizabeth called us afterward. She said that Kristy said Hurricane Bill had hit Sea City. Everybody was leaving the beach houses. The Pikes and the Barretts and the girls in the Baby-sitters Club were going to drive to a motel for the night.

After the call, Andrew looked scared. He went to the living room window and stared outside. "Is this the hurricane?" he asked.

"No, honey," Mommy answered. "Not yet."

Not *yet*? I guess that meant we were going to get it, too.

I stood near Andrew and looked outside. Rain was pouring down. The street was covered with water and tree branches. I couldn't imagine what a hurricane would look like. Poor Kristy.

The rest of the day I was dying to know what happened in Sea City. Did they find a place for all those people to stay in? Did the hurricane wreck any houses? Was anybody hurt?

I called Daddy's house after dinner, but the line was busy.

I called later and the line was still busy.

I called a third time and there was no answer.

I tried to call a fourth and fifth time, but there was not even a dial tone.

I went into the den. Seth, Mommy, and Andrew were watching the TV news. "The phone is not working," I said.

Seth nodded. "The lines are down all over Stoneybrook."

Boo, boo, boo. How was I going to find out about Kristy?

I sat down between Seth and Mommy on the couch. The newscasters were talking about damage to "coastal areas." We saw videos of smashed houses, waves crashing at people's front doors, cars up to their roofs in water, people rowing boats down *streets* covered with water.

"Is Sea City a coastal area?" I asked.

"Yes," Mommy replied.

"Did they say anything about it on the news?" I went on.

"They evacuated the beach," Seth answered. "That means everybody left their houses. Nobody's been hurt. That's the most important part. I'm sure Kristy is safe."

We watched some more. Then I asked, "Are *we* a coastal area?"

"Well, yes," Seth said.

"Does that mean Hurricane Bill is coming to Stoneybrook?"

Mommy put her arm around me. "Sometime late tonight or early tomorrow morning," she said. "If it stays on course."

"Oh."

"But we don't have a boat," Andrew said.

"We won't need one," Seth replied.

Andrew didn't seem convinced.

I don't know why I was not scared, but I wasn't. I was excited! I had never, ever been in a hurricane.

When a commercial came on, Seth stood up and said, "We better start preparing for this."

Andrew and I followed him into the pantry. He found a big roll of masking tape. Then he went from window to window and put tape on them in this pattern:

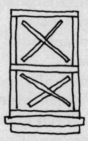

I helped him. Soon Mommy came in and helped, too.

Then we were ready. We watched some more news. After that Andrew and I were allowed to watch a video, since we couldn't go outside.

Then it was bedtime. I said good night to everyone and lay down in my bed. I read a little. I looked out the window. The rain was getting worse. The wind was howling.

Was *this* the hurricane?

I lay down again. I talked to Goosie a little (Goosie is my stuffed cat). I read some more. I thought about Kristy. I looked out the window again.

I did not sleep. At least I do not think I did.

All I know is that when the tree fell a little way down the block, I heard it. It went CRRRRRACCKK!

Then I heard Andrew scream. I ran into Mommy and Seth's room. Andrew was already in there, crying. "Is this it?" I asked.

"I think this may be it," Seth said.

We went downstairs to the kitchen. Seth turned on the radio. Mommy made some hot chocolate, even though it was the summer.

"Hurricane Bill is now sweeping through Stoneybrook," the radio man said. *"Fortunately, at this hour, there are few if any people on the street. The telephone company is still working to restore lines, although that won't happen for at least another day. The fire department is standing by for emergencies, and a few crews are already clearing debris from the main arteries . . ."*

"Clearing the Brie from someone's arteries?" I said.

I thought Seth and Mommy were going to fall over laughing. *"Debris* is stuff that's blown into the street. And that's what they mean by arteries — streets."

"Oh."

I looked at the stove clock and saw the time: 3:51. I couldn't believe it. I was staying up so late!

Our windows began to rattle like crazy. We

looked between the strips of tape, but we couldn't even see across the street. The rain was like a curtain. And the street was a river. It wasn't deep enough for a rowboat, though. (Boo.)

I don't know when I fell asleep. All I know is that when I woke up the next morning, I was in my bed.

And the sun was shining!

I looked outside. The front yard was a soggy mess. Branches were all over the place. Someone's mailbox was in a puddle on the sidewalk. The pavement on the street only showed through in the middle, because the gutters were full of water. A truck with a crane was parked at the corner. The crane reached to the top of a telephone pole, where someone was busily working.

Seth and Mommy were outside with a few neighbors, cleaning up. I got dressed and ran out to help.

"I knew those trees would fall someday!" someone was saying. "When they put in the curbs, they cut away the tree roots."

I looked down the street. There were three trees, small ones, that had fallen into the street. A fire department truck was pulling up beside the farthest one.

" 'Morning, sweetheart," Mommy said.

"The storm is over. No one was hurt. We just have some fallen trees, and a few power lines are down."

"Well, there'll be plenty of wood for winter!" our neighbor said.

Mommy and Seth laughed. I looked up at the telephone repair person.

All I could think about was Kristy. I hoped she was all right.

CHAPTER 21

Buddy

Thusday

Dear Daddy,
 Did you think the hericane got me? It didnt! Gues were we stayed? In a jim with a milion people. It was realy fun becase we had ice cream and the seeling did not leke. Now were back in are house and were CAMPING which is becase we have no elelctrisity!!!
 What a GRAT
 VACATION !!!!!!!!!!!!!!
 Your pal
 Buddy

Buddy

When I woke up, I forgot I was in the shelter. I thought I was at home. My bed at home is against the wall. So I rolled over and fell off the cot.

I landed on Mom.

"Aaaaah!" she screamed.

"Oh! Sorry!" I said.

Stacey woke up too, but Suzi and Marnie stayed asleep. So Stacey stayed with the Sleeping Uglies while Mom and I went to the cafeteria for breakfast. There was toast and jam. Also butter that was way too soft. And coffee. And fruit cocktail from big cans. But nothing else.

It was a pretty crummy breakfast.

Everybody woke up soon, even the Pikes. But I was the first one finished with breakfast. I ate three pieces of toast. I was still hungry, but I couldn't bear another piece.

Then the guy with the bullhorn came in and told us the sun was shining. We couldn't tell because of the boards covering the windows.

You should have heard the place. All these people clapped and cheered.

Soon Mom said, "Let's go before the rush."

We got out really fast, all twenty of us. Marnie stepped in a million puddles, but no one cared. When I did, Stacey and Mom yelled at me. Even though I was wearing my boots. That is so unfair.

We got in the car and drove to our house. It took SO LONG. I could have walked there faster.

As we drove along the main street, Mrs. Pike said, "Looks like we were lucky."

I didn't think so. The Ferris wheel hadn't fallen down. The store windows hadn't broken. No cars had crashed. No houses had blown away. No dead bodies were in the street. Nothing had happened.

It was *boring*.

When we reached the houses we saw *some* cool stuff. Shingles were missing on three roofs. A couple of houses did have broken windows, and someone's porch had collapsed.

Finally we got home. I wanted to play on the beach, until I got close to it.

What a disgusting mess. There were dead fish all over the place. Also soggy clothes and bottles and cans and trash. All the garbage cans were missing. Stacey said the fish were probably using them underwater. She's funny sometimes, for a baby-sitter.

We went inside. Everything was exactly where we had left it. But guess what? We had no electricity, even after Mom turned on the circus breakers. And when I went to get some water, the faucet spit at me! Then *brown* liquid came out, like smelly prune juice.

I filled a cup and tried to give it to Suzi. She

didn't think it was funny. And Mom and Stacey yelled at me again.

Soon we went over to the Pikes'. Margo and Vanessa told me we were going to go back to Stoneybrook. But they were lying.

Mr. Pike said, "Hey, we've been through the worst. I think we can tough it out the rest of the way."

All us kids said "Yeah!" So did the babysitters.

I thought Mom would want to go home, but even she wanted to stay. "It'll be fun," she said. "Cooking out everyday, reading by candlelight . . ."

So for two whole days, we had barbecue for breakfast, lunch, and dinner. Some neighbors started a group called Operation Recovery, and we joined. I helped a *policeman* pick up trash on the beach! He called me Buddy, even though he didn't know that was my name. That happens sometimes.

At night, we lit candles and told ghost stories. Dawn came over one night and told this scary one about Jared Mullray's girlfriend — who may still be in Dawn's barn!

I was really sad Friday night, because we had to leave Saturday. I think Mom knew how I felt. When she blew out my candle, she sat on my bed and whispered, "Are you okay?"

"You know," I answered, "I was scared

when Hurricane Bill came. But now I think it was the best thing about the vacation."

Mom laughed. "You were a great pioneer, Buddy."

"Yeah, like Davy Crockett."

Mom began to sing, "King of the Wild Frontierrrrr . . ."

I love that song. We sang together. I started feeling better. Then I drifted to sleep.

You know what? I decided something that night.

My mom is cool.

CHAPTER 22

LOGAN

FRIDAY

DEAR MARY ANNE,

WELCOME HOME. AS I WRITE THIS, I AM THINKING OF OUR NIGHT IN SEA CITY. REMEMBER WHEN WE WENT INTO THE HAUNTED HOUSE, AND THE LIGHTS WENT OUT? I PULLED YOU CLOSE. YOU PUT YOUR ARMS AROUND MY SHOULDER. WE TURNED TO EACH OTHER AND STARTED TO KISS.

IF THE ORANGE SLIME CREATURE HADN'T POPPED OUT OF THE WALL, IT WOULD HAVE BEEN A WONDERFUL MOMENT.

OH WELL. JUST THINK. NOW WE HAVE THE ENTIRE FALL TO SEARCH FOR EVEN MORE ROMANTIC MOMENTS. SOUND LIKE A GOOD IDEA?

I REALLY, REALLY MISSED YOU. I HOPE YOU LIKE THE SURPRISE I PLANNED.

LOVE,
YOUR HAPPY BOYFRIEND
LOGAN

200

"Hi, Terry, it's Logan," I said into the phone.

Terry is a new friend of mine. He's another busboy at the Rosebud Cafe. His parents run a big animal farm that's a tourist attraction in Mercer, Connecticut.

"Hi!" Terry said. "Listen, I talked to my dad about your idea for your girlfriend's welcome-home surprise."

"Yeah?"

"He wants to talk to you. I'll get him."

"Okay."

I waited patiently. It was Friday, and Mary Anne was coming back the next day. I wanted to do something really special for her.

I couldn't wait to see her. Especially after the week I'd had. It had been the absolute pits.

Why? Well, let me come right out and say it. From the moment I left Sea City, I couldn't stop thinking about Alex.

I know, I know. It sounds stupid, but there it is.

I had tried to put him out of my mind. I mean, he's just a *guy*. Just Mary Anne's friend.

But I kept thinking how much *free time* Mary Anne had in Sea City. Was she really going to want to spend it all with the same friends she saw every day in Stoneybrook? No way. I wouldn't if I were her.

Monday and Tuesday nights, I kept imagining her and Alex on the Sea City boardwalk. Each night I had this urge to call her — you know, just say hi, how are you. But I thought I might sound suspicious (well, I *was*). And what if she were out? I'd feel *worse*.

So I didn't call. Instead I just hoped she'd call me.

I didn't hear from her. Then Wednesday everyone was talking about Hurricane Bill. I began to feel really worried. I tried to call the Pikes' house, but no one answered.

I was going to try again on Thursday, but that was when the storm hit *us*. Our phone service went out.

When I finally got a dial tone, I called the operator. "Hello? Yes, I'm trying to reach Sea City. . . . No, *Sea* City. Excuse me? Service is still out? Okay, thank you."

"No luck?" Mom asked me.

"No," I replied glumly.

"Cheer up," Dad said. "The storm wasn't nearly as bad as they thought it would be. I'm sure they'll be okay."

"Yeah."

I knew Mary Anne was still there. If she'd escaped, she would have called immediately. The last postcard I'd received from her was dated Tuesday. She'd mentioned the storm at the very end, after a little section about Alex and Toby.

I figured they were on the island, too.

Great.

I kept trying to be realistic. There were probably a lot of people there. I tried to imagine where they would be. I had heard the houses were evacuated, and the electricity was out. People were probably huddled together somewhere. Maybe in one of the boardwalk shops. Maybe in the Haunted House.

I was *sure* Alex was with the Pikes. In a crisis, people always stick with other people they know.

I could just see it. No lights, everyone pulling together, singing songs and making the best of it. People arm in arm. Like a scene from a movie.

And in a dimly lit corner sit the hero and heroine. They hold hands and vow to brave it together. Then, as the singing swells and the candlelight flickers, they lean toward each other. . . .

Bruno, get a grip, I told myself.

At 9:45, the phone rang. "I'll get it!" I shouted.

I ran into the kitchen and picked it up. "Hello!"

"Hello, Logan? Ohhhhh, it's so good to hear

your voice. What a week! How are you?"

I was ecstatic. I was relieved. I was angry. I was hurt. So many complicated thoughts were running around in my head. But the only word I could manage was "Mary Anne?"

"Yes! Can you hear me okay?" she asked loudly.

"Fine!" I said. "Where are you?"

"Still in Sea City. Oh, I have so much to tell you when I get back. Guess what? They fixed the causeway a few hours ago."

"Wow, so you're going to come home — ?"

"Tomorrow, just the way we planned."

"That's great!" I said. "But — but how is everyone? No one got hurt?"

"No. Everyone's fine. I mean, the storm was scary. But we've had the *best* time!"

"And all your neighbors and friends? You know, Toby and Alex, for instance."

Ugh. Very subtle, Bruno.

"They're fine. We saw them today for the first time all week. They spent the storm inland. Their cars were the last ones to make it over the causeway before the flood."

"Oh," I said. "Hmm, how lucky. . . . "

Whoa. Did I feel stupid. Idiotic. Off the scale on the Dorkometer.

I was glad Mary Anne could not see the color of my face.

One whole week of guessing and second-guessing. Worrying and suspecting and assuming. I guess I *should* have felt ecstatic. (Well, I did, sort of.) But it was almost a letdown. I mean, all that worrying had been a lot of work — and for nothing!

We had a great phone call. I didn't mention a word about how I'd felt. I just let myself steep in guilt, like a tea bag.

That was when I had the urge to give Mary Anne something really special as a welcome-home present. And Terry Dutton's dad came to mind.

So that brings me to Friday. There I was, waiting for Terry's dad to come on the phone.

"Hi, are you Terry's friend?" he asked.

"Yes, sir," I said.

"What's this idea Terry tells me about?"

I described my plan to him. It was a little wacky, and I thought he'd say no.

He listened to every word, and then said, "Young man, that is the craziest idea I ever heard — "

"I'm sorry to take up your time, sir," I cut in. "Thank you for — "

"And I love it!" he continued. "Sounds like the kind of thing I used to do with Terry's mom when we were young."

"R-really?" I said.

"You don't think we had any spunk when we were young?"

"No! I mean, yes! I mean, I'm sure you did. It's just — "

He laughed. "All right, Logan. Let's figure out a time of delivery and return, and I'll take care of the rest."

I couldn't believe he had said yes. Mary Anne was going to be thrilled out of her mind!

CHAPTER 23

Mallory

Friday

Dear Diary,
   Did I make the right decision? I think so.
When I look back and read this, I will say,
"Mallory Pike, you showed courage and
maturity."
   Either that or, "Whoa, were you out of
your mind?"
   No, I doubt that.
   Let me start at the beginning.
   Today was my Big Date with Toby....

mallory

ॐ

My heart was fluttering the minute I woke up. I threw aside my covers. I ran to the mirror.

Left side of face. Right side of face. No pimples. Good.

It had not been a great summer, blemish-wise. When you're as fair as I am, your skin can do weird things in the heat. Blisters, pimples, heat rashes, you name it.

But not this morning. Not the morning of the evening of the Big Date.

Okay. Hair. Horrendous as usual. Thick and frizzy and piled up on one side from sleeping. A cross between Bozo the Clown and the Bride of Frankenstein (Frankenstein the Clown? The Bride of Bozo?) But I could deal with that.

I found my brush and did my ritual morning arm wrestle with my hair. I managed to control it enough to trap it with some hair clips.

Then I pinched my cheeks, said, "Good morning, beautiful," and went downstairs.

This was not like me.

In case you haven't noticed, I am not Ms. Fashion-and-Glamour of the Baby-sitters Club. (More like Ms. Braces-and-Glasses.) But I was meeting *him* tonight.

What would I wear? Should I put on makeup? Could I learn *how* to put on makeup in time? Should I practice what to say? Should I leave my glasses home?

I was beginning to realize what it must be like to be Stacey.

Uh, no. *Not* a good comparison. For one thing, I wasn't feeling mean and jealous.

Which was how Stacey had been acting for days. She had hardly said a word to me. When she did, she made sure it was something nasty.

At first I felt confused and hurt. But not any more. By Friday I was determined to have a fun, relaxing day.

If I could keep myself from exploding with anticipation.

So I bounced downstairs and cried, "Good morning!"

As usual, Jessi was already up, making pancakes and eggs and bacon.

"Listen, Mallory!" Adam exclaimed. He was grinning broadly. "I one my mother . . . I two my mother . . . I three my mother . . . I four my mother . . . I five my mother . . ."

My siblings were chanting along with him now. I could see where this was leading.

"I six my mother . . . I seven my mother . . . I EIGHT MY MOTHER!"

They erupted with laughter. "Get it?" Adam said. "I *ate* my mother!"

Mallory
☺

I tried very hard not to laugh. It would only encourage him. "Adam, eat your pancakes," I replied.

When the kids had finished, my friends and I sat down to breakfast. "Are you ready?" Jessi asked me with a sly grin.

"Actually," I said, "I was thinking of going into town to get some barrettes, maybe a fun kind of pin . . ."

"I'll go with you!" Claudia volunteered.

"Me too!" Jessi said.

"Don't worry about the kids," Mary Anne added. "We'll take care of them."

What great friends. "Okay!" I said. "Thanks!"

Well, Claudia and Jessi and I had the best time. Claudia found me a pair of barrettes in the shape of flamingoes — but cool, not corny-looking. Then we bought about ten tiny buttons with pictures on them. The faces included Virginia Woolf, Jimi Hendrix, Stephen Hawking, and Janis Joplin, but Claud didn't know who any of them were. She just picked them because they looked "funky."

On the way back, guess who we ran into?

Stacey was taking the Barrett kids to the boardwalk for ice cream. "Hi," she said.

"Hi," Jessi and Claudia answered.

"Where've you been?" Stacey asked.

"Shopping," I said, clutching my bag a little tighter.

"Ooh, can I see?"

I felt awkward. I didn't want to be rude, so I opened the bag for her.

"Wow . . . really *interesting*," Stacey said. "Is this stuff for Margo and Vanessa?"

"No," I replied, grabbing the bag back. "It happens to be for me."

"Well, ex*cuuuuuse* me," Stacey shot back. She began shoving the Barrett kids ahead of her. "I guess we'll see you all later."

When we were far enough away, I said, "See? She hates me."

Jessi sighed and shook her head. "I just don't understand what's going on between you two."

We walked back to the house. "Claudia," I said, "do you think I should wear jeans and a polo shirt with this stuff, or something fancier?"

"Show me what you have," Claudia replied, "and we'll figure out something."

The three of us ran inside and upstairs. We pulled out just about every outfit I had brought.

Claudia took a look at everything. Then she made Jessi take out *her* outfits.

I tried on casual. I tried on fancy. I tried on

weird combinations. I just followed the directions of Claudia Kishi, Fashion Consultant.

As I slipped on a clingy, short sundress, I heard high-pitched squeaks behind me.

Mice? No, Pikes.

Jessi opened the door. Adam, Jordan, and Nicky fell into the room. "Hrrrrumph!" Jessi said.

They scrambled to their feet. "Oh, um, we were — ha ha — looking for Nicky's Etch-a-Sketch," Adam said.

Claudia glanced around. "Hmmm, doesn't seem to be here in Jessi and Mal's room."

"Okay, 'bye!" The boys were off like a shot. We could hear them giggling as they ran down the stairs. Then: "Mal and Toby sitting in a tree, N-E-C-K-I-N-G!"

"Boys!" my dad's voice bellowed.

"Now, where were we?" Claudia said.

We worked for another half an hour. I ended up choosing a short, flared, white-on-blue polka-dotted skirt (mine); a white, ribbed tank-top (Jessi's); and a long, royal-blue men's shirt with the tails tied in front (Claudia had run to *her* room for that). Claudia insisted I not wear anything too light or it would "wash out my face." We carefully placed some of the buttons we'd bought on the tanktop.

Claudia yanked back my mane and figured

out how to put the flamingo barrettes in it so they wouldn't get lost.

I looked in the mirror. I watched a smile light up my own face. "Wow! I look pretty good."

"Pretty good?" Claudia repeated. "You look *sensational*! Toby's eyes are going to fall out!"

"That ought to be an interesting date," Jessi remarked.

I sighed. "Doesn't this remind you of the time you helped me dress for the Valentine Dance?"

Claudia laughed. "After you'd had that big fight with Ben — over how to use the *library card catalog*?"

Ben.

I really hadn't thought of him. Ben Hobart was the only boy I ever went out with before this trip. We'd been to the movies, and just about all of the school dances. I'd never officially called him my boyfriend or anything, though.

So why was I feeling this sudden twinge of guilt?

"Remember when you went to the movie theater with the little cafe?" Jessi asked.

I cringed. "And I poured sugar on the popcorn!"

We laughed. And I felt this incredible urge to call Ben. I really *missed* him.

I put aside my outfit and changed into beach clothes. Then I told Jessi and Claudia I'd meet them outside, and I went into my parents' room.

I still remembered Ben's number.

"Hello, Hobart residence."

Mr. Hobart's voice made me break into a smile. The Hobarts are from Australia and speak with this wonderful accent. "Hi, Mr. Hobart! This is Mallory!"

"Well, hello, love! Let me get Ben for you!"

In a second, Ben was on the phone. "Hi, Mallory!"

Hoi, Mel-ry! Oh, was that great! He sounded thrilled. "Hi, Ben. How are you?"

"Alive." *Aloiv.* "I guess you survived the storm, huh? We lost a tree. It missed our car by about five inches!"

We talked and talked and talked. We didn't stop until we'd filled in the past two weeks. I found out that Johnny Hobart had turned on all the flashlights the night before the storm "to warm them up." Of course, their block was the only one to lose power in the hurricane. Then Ben told me how Mathew went to grab "a cocoon" in the branch of the tree that fell in the street — and it turned out to be a sleeping bat.

It was the funniest, happiest conversation

I'd had in a long time. I didn't want to hang up.

When I did, I realized something.

There was no one I wanted to go out with but Ben.

I tried to get excited about my date with Toby again. But I just couldn't. The thrill was completely gone.

I walked slowly downstairs, in a daze. Then I went to the beach and spent the rest of the afternoon with everyone. Later I talked to Jessi about it.

"Look," she said, "it's up to you. What time is he picking you up?"

"Seven o'clock."

Jessi looked at her watch. "You have an hour. This is your last day in Sea City. Do whatever makes you happy."

"But my mind is so mixed up," I said.

"Well, don't do it from your mind, then. Do it from your heart."

I giggled. "Jessi, that's corny."

She laughed, too. "It's true, though."

Jessi is so smart.

The beach was starting to get that cool, late afternoon feeling. All the Pikes and Barretts were playing extra hard, building extra nice castles, taking extra long swims.

I was going to miss this place so much.

Maybe it would be best just to spend the last day with my friends and family.

"You decided not to go on your date?"

Leave it to Stacey McGill to destroy a wonderful mood.

I turned to look at her. "I didn't say that."

Stacey shrugged. "Sorry. It was just getting late. I thought maybe you'd come to your senses."

That did it.

"For your information, I *am* going. In fact, I was just heading back to the house now."

I stormed away. There was no way I'd give Stacey the satisfaction of thinking she changed my mind!

I marched straight to my room and put on my outfit. Then I waited on the porch, pacing back and forth.

Toby arrived at seven. He was smiling as he walked to the porch. And he looked gorgeous.

But the side of me that wanted to go was saying: *Stacey will be so jealous.* And the rest of me was saying, *I wish Ben were here.*

"You look great, cutie!" Toby said, stepping onto the porch.

I smiled. I looked him in the eye.

Do it from the heart, Jessi had said. Some-

how, that silly little statement made things much clearer.

"Toby," I said. "Um, I feel really embarrassed about something. Can we . . . uh, talk?"

He shrugged. "We are talking."

Go for it, I told myself. "Toby, I know I should have said this earlier, but I have this boyfriend at home. His name is Ben, and . . . well, we're kind of going steady."

Toby's smile disappeared. "Oh. Well, I didn't know. . . ."

"You couldn't have. I'm really sorry. You came all the way over here and everything. But, I guess I was just so *amazed* you'd even be interested in me. I mean, you're a really cute guy and all . . ."

"I can't convince you to go out just as a friend?"

I shook my head. "It's my family's last evening here. I think I'm going to spend it with them."

Toby sighed and looked down. "Well, I guess I understand. I mean, if I had a steady girl I'd do the same."

"Thanks," I said.

Toby forced a smile. "Well, have a fun time. If you come back next summer and know of another cute girl who's unattached, let me know, okay?"

Huh?

"Okay," I said. " 'Bye, Toby."

" 'Bye, Mal."

I went back into the house to change. I dragged myself up the stairs. Walking down the hallway to my room, I was lost in thought. I had ruined Toby's night, and that didn't seem fair. But that *comment* he made! Was that all I was to him, just "another cute girl"?

I flung open my door.

Stacey was sitting on the bed.

I stared at her. "For your information, Toby did not dump me," I said. "That's not why I'm back so soon."

Stacey looked as if she were about to cry. "Oh, Mallory, I'm sorry . . . about everything."

All my anger melted away. Stacey stood up, and we gave each other a big, big hug. "It's okay," I said.

"No, it's not," Stacey replied. "I was a jerk. For some reason, I was jealous that Toby liked *you*, when he had dumped *me*. I just talked to Jessi about it. I — I don't want to be enemies. A boy isn't worth that. You can do whatever you want."

"I already did," I said. "And I'll tell you about it at the barbecue tonight."

"You — you're staying?"

I nodded. "But not looking like this. Mind if I change?"

Mallory

For the first time in two weeks, I saw a smile cross Stacey's face.

I took the flamingoes from my hair and started thinking about spare ribs. This was my last night in Sea City, and I planned to have some *fun*!

EPILOGUE

Dear Alex,

You know what
was waiting for me
at the Pikes' house
when we got home?
A horse and buggy.
A real one! Logan
had hired it to
take me home!!

Oh, I thought I
was going to pass out.
It was so romantic.
We threw my luggage
in and clopped down
the street. The Pikes,
the Barretts, and my
friends all cheered as
we rode away.

Logan's friend
Terry was the driver,
and he kept trying
to tell jokes. But I

didn't mind a bit.
 I will never forget
this my whole life.
            Sincerely,
            Mary Anne
P.S. How was your
    trip back?
P.P.S. Good luck with
  baseball season,
    whenever it starts.

Hi daddy,
   Were back and its much
more boring here. Nicky
did not thro up on the way
back. Momy and stacy had
a long talk and mom kept
sayig she was sory about
somthing i dont kno what.
But they were cereus for a
long time and then real
freindly. We playd lots of
gams until Marny becam a
pan in the you kno what.
   WRIGHT BACK!!!!!!!!!!!!
            Buddy

222

Dear Keisha,
   Being a Super
Sitter isn't all it's
cracked up to be.
Next year I'll
cut back to
Regular Sitter status.
I need a
vacation.
                    Love
                    Jessi

Dear Granny and Grandad,
   My stepsister Kristy came home. She was in the
hurricane, too. But Sea City had it worse than we
did. It flooded a whole long road. It knocked out all
the electricity. It damaged big houses.
   But it didn't do a thing to Kristy. She's tough.
                          Love, Karen

Dear Dad,
   How was the hurricane in the Big
Apple? Did any skyscrapers blow
away? We all survived. Details when
I see you this weekend.

Remember I told you about Toby, that guy who dumped me? Well, he tried to pick up Mallory Pike. Yes, Mallory Pike. She fell for him at first, but then decided to remain true to Ben Hobart. I was really proud of her. I was thinking of inviting her along when I come to New York. Would it be Ok?

Luv, Stace

FIRST GLASS, INC.
GLAZIERS & WINDOW DESIGN

Mr. and Mrs. Pike
10 Slate Street
Stoneybrook, CT
Dear Mr. and Mrs. Pike,
This is to confirm our appointment for this Saturday at 10:00 A.M. for the replacement of two (2) broken living room windows, one (1) basement window, and one (1) bedroom window. Due to the unexpected extent of storm damage to glass in your neighborhood, we were unable to make the appointment at an earlier date.

Sincerely,

Robert Thompson

Robert Thompson
Manager

Dear Kristy,
We are still on vacation. don't kick us of the team ok. We still want to play. even if the other players you got were realy good.
From,
Jake Kuhn

CAMP AZURE HILLS

Hi, Claudia!
Are you home yet? What a summer you must have had! I heard about Hurricane Bill. We missed it completely up here.
So, now that you're all home with nothing to do for a couple of weeks, how about a BSC trip to see a fellow member in Oklahoma?
Maybe you could come with the Pikes and the Barretts?
Oh, well, think about it.
Love, Shannon

Dear Pike Family,

Thank you so much for your good nature and perseverence during our weather emergency. You took wonderful care of the house, and damage was negligible. Other realtors were not so lucky (*I* was not so lucky in some cases).

I will be happy to hold the house open for you next summer. I'm sure it will be a sunny, perfect August!

Sincerely,

Ellen Cooke

Ellen Cooke

Dear Mallory,
I just want you to know, I'm not mad at you at all. In fact, I'm kind of glad you did what you did. If you hadn't, it would have been an uncomfortable date.

you have a steady
boyfriend and that's
cool. So I guess you
wouldn't mind sending
me the address of
your friend Jessi?
She seemed very
nice. How old is she?
Is she seeing some-
one?
　　Hope to hear soon.
　　　　Toby

About the Author

ANN M. MARTIN did *a lot* of baby-sitting when she was growing up in Princeton, New Jersey. She is a former editor of books for children, and was graduated from Smith College.

Ms. Martin lives in New York City with her cats, Mouse and Rosie. She likes ice cream and *I Love Lucy*; and she hates to cook.

Ann Martin's Apple Paperbacks include *Yours Turly, Shirley*; *Ten Kids, No Pets*; *With You and Without You*; *Bummer Summer*; and all the other books in the Baby-sitters Club series.

THE BABY-SITTERS CLUB®

by Ann M. Martin

More titles... ▶

The Baby-sitters Club titles continued...

Available wherever you buy books...or use this order form.

Scholastic Inc., P.O. Box 7502, 2931 E. McCarty Street, Jefferson City, MO 65102

Please send me the books I have checked above. I am enclosing $———
(please add $2.00 to cover shipping and handling). Send check or money order - no
cash or C.O.D.s please.

Name ————————————————————————————

Address ————————————————————————————

City———————————————— State/Zip ————————————
Please allow four to six weeks for delivery. Offer good in the U.S. only. Sorry, mail orders are not
available to residents of Canada. Prices subject to change.

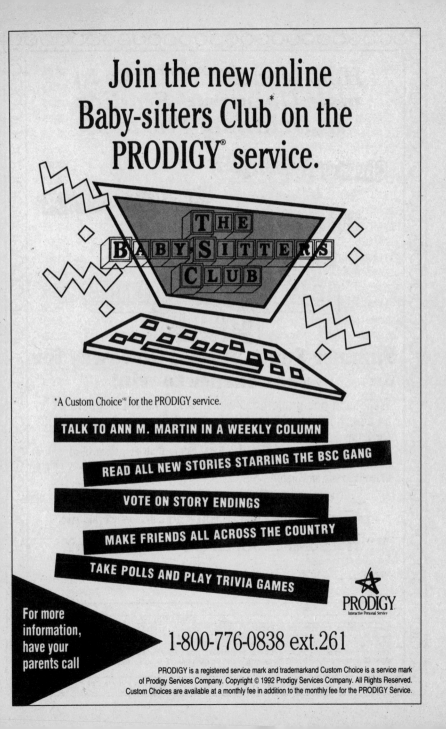

Join the new online Baby-sitters Club* on the PRODIGY® service.

*A Custom Choice℠ for the PRODIGY service.

TALK TO ANN M. MARTIN IN A WEEKLY COLUMN

READ ALL NEW STORIES STARRING THE BSC GANG

VOTE ON STORY ENDINGS

MAKE FRIENDS ALL ACROSS THE COUNTRY

TAKE POLLS AND PLAY TRIVIA GAMES

PRODIGY
Interactive Personal Service

For more information, have your parents call

1-800-776-0838 ext.261

How would YOU like to visit Universal Studios in Orlando, Florida?

Check out the sights!

Experience the rides!

Tour the Studios!

Enter THE BABY-SITTERS CLUB®

Summer Super Special Giveaway for your chance to win!

We'll send one grand prize winner and a parent or guardian on an all expense paid trip to Universal Studios in Orlando, Florida for 3 days and 2 nights!

25 second prize winners receive a Baby-sitters Club Fun Pack filled with a Baby-sitters Club T-Shirt, "Songs For My Best Friends" cassette, Baby-sitters Club stationery and more!

All you have to do is fill out the coupon below or write the information on a 3" x 5" piece of paper and mail to:

THE BABY-SITTERS CLUB SUMMER SUPER SPECIAL GIVEAWAY P.O. Box 7500, Jefferson City, MO 65102. Return by November 30 1993.

- -

THE SUMMER SUPER SPECIAL GIVEAWAY

Name_____ Birthdate _____

Address_____

City_____ State/Zip _____

Rules: Entries must be postmarked by November 30, 1993. Winners will be picked at random and notified by mail. No purchase necessary. Valid only in the U.S. Void where prohibited. Taxes on prizes are the responsibility of the winners and their immediate families. Employees of Scholastic Inc; its agencies, affiliates, subsidiaries, and their immediate families not eligible. For a complete list of winners, send a self-addresses stamped envelope to: The Baby-sitters Club Summer Super Special Giveaway, Winners List, after November 30 at the address provided above.

BSC693